# Smitten in the Stacks

## FOR THE LOVE OF AUSTEN

SHERRY SINCLAIR

EVER AFTER INK

# Books by Sherry Sinclair

For the Love of Austen Series (sweet romance)

*The Sweetest Ingredient*

*Smitten in the Stacks*

*Pride & Property*

Stand-Alone Novels (Semi-Steamy romance)

*Romance, Lies, & Sorority Ties*

If you want to be notified when Sherry Sinclair's next novel is released or whenever she's offering free reads, please sign up for her newsletter to be notified of new releases, giveaways, and free reads by clicking: https://dashboard.mailerlite.com/forms/748734/109192166606112621/share (*Your email will never be shared, and you can unsubscribe at any time.*)

And please join Sherry's Facebook group to discuss the romance genre, life, and swap book recommendations: https://www.facebook.com/groups/authorsherrysinclair

Follow Sherry Sinclair on Facebook - Twitter – TikTok – Instagram

SMITTEN IN THE STACKS

Ever After Ink Publications

First Edition June 13, 2024



Cover art by The Cover Coven and TMT Book Cover Design

# Dedication

*Dedicated to (me!) the hopeless romantic within, who never tires of spinning tales of love and humor.*

*To the vocal cast of characters in my head, who incessantly demand their romances be shared with the world (okay, okay, you got your wish!).*

*And to my amazing family and cat crew (the purr-fect support system!), who've provided endless inspiration, encouragement, and lots of cuddles throughout my writing career.*

# Foreword

Dear Readers,

I'm excited to share with you my series of standalone novels affectionately titled, *For the Love of Austen*, that are lighthearted romantic tales with a nod to Jane Austen's works in each book, some a little more than others.

Jane Austen once wrote, "There is nothing like staying at home for real comfort."

So, consider this series my invitation to you to find the coziest nook in your home, pour a cup of tea, or perhaps a tasty mug of coffee, and prepare to embark on a journey that intertwines romance and heartfelt moments with a slice of humor.

Whether you are a Janeite through and through, or simply love fluffy, feel-good stories that end with a satisfying kiss, there is something for you to enjoy. No cliffhangers and plenty of heart, humor, and Happy-Ever-Afters in each book.

Sincerely,
*Sherry*

# Smitten in the Stacks

# Chapter One

AS THE SELF-PROCLAIMED BIBLIOPHILE QUEEN OF Bluebell Bend, I wielded my weapons—barcode scanner, pastry, and matchmaking skills—with pride. My bookshop, *Prose & Positivity*, specialized in romance, where I got to ogle hot guys on book covers and play literary Cupid.

Sushi, my fluffy white Persian, reclined on the highest shelf like she owned the place (she did). Her judgmental stare tracked my every move.

I set down a plate of tuna on the counter. "Afternoon, Your Highness."

*Yes*, she only ate restaurant-grade fish. *No*, I had no idea how this happened.

The shop's furry diva hopped down and ate her meal.

"Time to prep for the book club meeting."

Her tail twitched in acknowledgment or perhaps mild annoyance—I was never quite sure which.

I got busy arranging chairs into a circle near the counter. It was Sunday afternoon, and the only day the bookshop was closed. The highlight of my month was hosting the Literary Persuasion Society book club. A day when my friends came together to dissect and debate our latest reads.

While I waited for the members to arrive, I shuffled across the room in high-top sneakers that added exactly zero inches to my five-foot-three stature, still glitter-splattered from last week's marketing campaign—*don't ask*. In the kitchenette, I fired up the coffee machine, brewing java so strong it could fuel a nuclear reactor—or at least ignite a lively discussion on a good enemies-to-lovers trope.

Returning to the main area, I found a pile of paperbacks had fallen over. No doubt courtesy of Sushi.

My hands trembled as I restacked the books by a certain author who shall remain nameless. With a shaky breath, I straightened. I would not let my mind wander to the foolishness I had once fallen for—hook, line, and sinker, just like poor Marianne Dashwood.

Sushi bumped her head against my hand, a reminder that I was unconditionally loved. I petted her fur, then slipped my phone from my pocket to check my Instagram persona.

Ah, the glamorous life of a wannabe book influencer.

Scrolling through my latest posts, admiring the artfully arranged stacks of novels and the cleverly crafted captions that I hoped would inspire others to appreciate the wonderful world of romance.

Sure, my current audience consisted mostly of my aunt Margo, a few loyal customers, and my best friend, Rachel. But I had big dreams, dreams of becoming the go-to girl for all things romance, of changing lives one book recommendation at a time.

I glanced at my cat. "*Hmmm*, do our followers want more live dramatic readings of classic literature? Or should we post more photos of us, looking all extra cute?"

"Meow." Her insistent tone reverberated through the quiet bookstore.

"More cat photos, you say? You little narcissist."

"Meow."

"Fine, fine. One quick selfie. First I need to get camera worthy."

I tried twisting my hair into a bun, but the end result looked more unfashionably messy than haute couture. Sighing, I straightened my graphic tee with the phrase, '*Proud Book Nerd,*' worn with my favorite skinny jeans.

Ah yes, my signature look—casual chic with a side of bookish rebellion.

Scooping up Sushi, she snuggled over my shoulder, a content purr vibrating against my chest. We posed together —a woman, her bookstore, and her cat—framed by the backdrop of vibrantly colored bookshelves.

When the photoshoot ended, she hopped down, sashayed over to the counter, and vaulted onto the surface.

The chime above the door announced Aunt Margo's arrival, her presence like a burst of spicy incense. As my only relative who lived in town, she held a special place in my life, while my parents enjoyed retirement in Florida.

My aunt flounced up to the counter draped in her usual ensemble of paisley and turquoise, the jingle of her bracelets competing with the wind chimes outside. Her tall figure and olive complexion were offset by the long mane of silver hair.

"Paris, honey." Aunt Margo stroked Sushi's fur, sending white tufts into the air. "Have you checked your horoscope? Venus is in transit, and that means—"

"Love is on the horizon?" I rolled my eyes. "You've been saying that since I was sixteen, Aunt Margo."

She peered at me over her reading glasses. "And one day

I'll be right." She threw head back and laughed. Her laughter was as warm as the sunlight streaming through the windows. "This time, I have not-so-great news. Your horoscope's indicating a severe love drought."

As much as I adored my hometown, the dating pool was more of a dried-up water stain. I'd mentally swiped left on every bachelor within a ten-mile radius—*twice*.

The issue wasn't a lack of dates, it was that no one understood my desire for an epic, sweep-me-off-my-feet love affair. In many ways, I was the stereotypical single girl whose closest relationships were with a judgy furball who hogged my pillow and Jane Austen.

"Perhaps you were too quick to dismiss Barry."

My aunt's last hopeful for me was the town's butcher, known for his love of meat puns and an unsettling habit of talking to his sausages as if they were his offspring.

I smiled wryly at my aunt. "He's a nice guy, but not my type. And while I appreciate your efforts to help me find love, I'm not sure playing matchmaker is your forte."

Aunt Margo sniffed. "I thought Barry was perfect for you."

"I'm not sure I want to be with someone who's more emotionally invested in his venison than in me."

Aunt Margo grinned. "Whatever do you mean? He even gave you that lovely bouquet of beef jerky. Now that's a man who knows how to express his feelings."

"Yes, because nothing says romance like cured meat. I just don't want to settle for someone who thinks a romantic dinner involves a candlelit display of cold cuts."

"What about the nice boy who works at the hardware store? He seems to have a thing for you."

I frowned. "You mean the one who smells like WD-40 and asked me if I wanted to see his wrench collection?"

She threw her hands up. "Heavens, Paris! At this rate, you'll end up a spinster with nothing but your books and Sushi for company."

"At least neither tries to woo me with processed meats or power tools." I wandered over to the Jane Austen first editions. "How can I settle for a guy who thinks dried meat sticks are the height of romance when I have a literary hero like Mr. Knightley who knows how to court a woman with wit, charm, and impeccable manners?"

"You and your romantic notions. You even spurned the delightful English major in thrifted corduroys and elbow patches I tried to set you up with." My aunt clucked her tongue. "You have to give *real* men a chance, flaws and all. Like my third husband. The man couldn't even butter toast without causing a culinary disaster, but I adored him."

With a practiced air of nonchalance, I shrugged off her concern. "I'm not looking for Mr. Perfect. I just want someone who gets me, who loves me for *me*...like Darcy from *Bridget Jones's Diary*. And besides, at least fictional guys never hog the blankets or leave their dirty socks on the floor."

Aunt Margo shook her head. "Why are you so set against giving anyone a chance? It can't just be because of your fascination for fictitious heroes."

The sudden pain of the past resurfaced like a fresh, unhealed wound. "Do you, uh, remember last year when Julian Hale did a book signing here?"

She frowned. "The handsome, tweed-clad wordsmith of those racy historical romances?"

"That's him. Well, I...had a fling with Julian last summer." A sharp pang pierced my chest. "He was charming, insightful, and he understood my passion for literature. Except he wasn't the person I thought he was. Turns out,

Julian was engaged to someone else, and I was just a minor subplot." My fingers absently traced the spine of a nearby book. "I'm just protecting myself from getting hurt again."

Blinking back tears threatening to smudge my carefully applied mascara, I tried to squash the memory of that ill-fated romance. The wounds of my past heartbreak were still raw, and perhaps that's why I found solace in the pages of my books, where the heroines never had to avoid Willoughby-*esque* suitors, survive disastrous blind dates, or step on hairballs.

She squeezed my hand. "One idiot's mistake shouldn't cast a shadow over the entire male species." Her expression softened. "Don't let one experience define you or make you judge all men by his actions. You're wiser, stronger, and more deserving of happiness than ever before."

My mouth dried. Could Aunt Margo be right? Was I holding out for a literary ideal that didn't exist outside the pages of books?

"How do you know when it's someone worth taking a chance on?"

Aunt Margo reached out to tuck a stray lock of hair behind my ear. "When someone makes you feel like you're the leading lady in your own love story, that's when you'll know."

I gave her an affectionate peck on the cheek. "One can hope. If I ever do find someone special, I'll try not to let my cynicism get in the way."

The bell above the entrance jingled merrily and we turned as the door swung open.

My best friend Rachel Graham breezed inside, her entrance heralded by the aroma of cranberries and oranges even before I spotted the tray of baked sweets she carried. Rachel enjoyed providing the refreshments, and I appreciated her baking skills almost as much as I appreciated her friendship.

After all, what's a book club without a little sugar to sweeten the bitter taste of unrequited love?

"Am I interrupting the latest astrological forecast?" Rachel was a petite biracial woman with light-brown skin and dark curls styled in a ponytail. She had an effortless style, wearing a pink sweater over chinos with glaringly white kicks, making her look like she had just stepped out of a spring-themed catalogue.

Aunt Margo's kohl-rimmed blue eyes lit up. "No, just ensuring our Paris here is ready for all the love the universe has in store."

"Of course she is." Rachel gave me a warm smile.

"Those smell delicious." I was already drooling.

Rachel placed her baked goods beside the gurgling coffeepot. I snagged a sugary scone, biting into the soft, spiced dough, then groaned.

Aunt Margo leaned over, her voice low, teasing. "Actually, Paris and I were debating on whether any man has ever made her heart skip a beat outside of literature."

Rachel nudged my aunt with her elbow. "Ah, but what's wrong with bookish affairs? I might be a married lady, but there's always room for a fictional fling or two."

"Or three, or four," I said.

Grinning, Aunt Margo turned to me and her gaze slid over my head. "That new hair color is quite the statement."

Maybe it was her polite way of saying I stood out more than I blended in, an outsider among the conventional hairstyles and humdrum fashion trends that populated Bluebell Bend.

Flicking hair over my shoulder, I shrugged. "Just needed a change."

Rachel slanted her head. "It's bold, like her taste in books. Not everyone can pull off discussing classics like *Mansfield Park* with the same enthusiasm as the novel *Fifty Shades of Beige*."

Aunt Margo shook her head. "You truly are one of a kind, honey. And Bluebell Bend is lucky to have you, even if they don't always understand you."

"Well, I like to think of myself as the town's very own Emma Woodhouse. Matchmaking books with readers, one happily ever after at a time."

My heart turned over heavily. Their fondness for my quirkiness was like a gentle reminder of the fine line I walked between my world and others. In my bookstore, surrounded by tales of love and escapism, I was the town's book cupid. Beyond these walls, I was Paris Novak, the girl with the quirky tees, purple hair, and mismatched socks, always one step out of sync with the rhythm of Bluebell Bend.

The door opened and Samuel Smith, an African-American man in his forties, with brown eyes peering behind square-framed glasses, walked inside.

"Hello, everyone!" Samuel said in a loud, booming voice. "I've got some opinions about our latest read." He sat in one of the chairs.

Pouring myself a mug of coffee, I smiled at the way his polyester tartan pants and polo shirt looked like he'd just stepped off the driving range.

Our final member, Carmen Flores, a Hispanic widow in her fifties, made her entrance moments later. "Good afternoon!" Her dark-brown hair rested on slender shoulders, and she wore a batik print top over linen pants.

Samuel cleared his throat. "Prepare yourselves for a

fresh perspective. I've invited a friend to join our literary gathering. He's running late, but should be here soon."

I nearly choked on my coffee. *A new member?*

Slumping in my seat, I cast a wary glance at the door. Our group had been a close-knit circle for so long that the thought of someone else joining our book club was mildly panic-inducing.

Was I ready to let some random stranger join our book discussions and into my life?

*No.* No, I wasn't. About as ready as I was to swap my cherished paperbacks for eBooks—nostalgically resistant and slightly appalled. Change and I had never been on good terms, and I wasn't about to start embracing it now.

# Chapter Two

Around me, the Literary Persuasion Society members found their spots, lounging in the mismatched chairs placed in a circle on the hardwood floor.

"Did everyone enjoy this month's book pick?" Aunt Margo sat beside Samuel, flipping through her well-worn copy.

"I devoured it," Samuel admitted. "Those plot twists? *Chef's kiss!*"

Sushi, the club's furry mascot, paraded around, soaking up adoration like a miniature, fur-coated monarch.

"Careful now, Samuel, your inner romantic is showing," I teased, sipping my coffee.

Rachel tilted her head. "Nothing wrong with a man appreciating a good love story."

"I agree," Carmen said. "It's the language of the human heart, after all."

My gaze drifted over my assembled friends who were more like family to me, making being single in Bluebell Bend a little less lonely.

Glancing out the large front window at Bluebell Bend

in springtime, it appeared as picture-perfect as a feel-good Hallmark movie. And I wasn't just saying that because I owned the pinkest building on Main Street, complete with gingerbread woodwork and baby blue shutters. There were blooming gardens, neat brick buildings, locals chatting over steamy cups of hot chocolate at the café across the street, and bright blue skies.

Movement caught my eye and I turned my head. Sushi launched a tactical assault on a stack of bookmarks on the counter, spilling them on the floor.

I set my coffee on the counter. "Bad kitty."

Sushi blinked at me unapologetically and leaped down.

Squatting, I gathered the bookmarks off the floor. My reflection glanced back at me from the glass display case—big blue eyes and a pale oval-shaped face that could use a touch more sleep and a smidge less stress.

Just as I straightened, the door burst open with a loud thud, startling everyone. A yelp escaped my lips and the bookmarks in my hand took flight, soaring upward before fluttering down around me like oversized confetti.

I recognized the newcomer as Daxton Granger, a personal trainer and the talk of every gym-goer in Bluebell Bend. Of course, I'd only heard about him through the grapevine, since the closest I'd come to a gym was watching Netflix while lounging on my yoga mat.

Dax walked inside and shut the door, the human embodiment of a romance novel cover, looking like he could bench press the entire historical section, his biceps straining under his snug T-shirt. And let's be real—at thirty-years-old, my soft, slender figure was less about hitting the weights and more about nibbling on sugary pastries.

Who needed washboard abs when I could deadlift a hardback? I'd take a good book over a treadmill any day.

"Sorry, I'm late." Dax wore a grin, equal parts charm and arrogance. "Got held up at work."

Carmen smiled at Dax. "Welcome to the Literary Persuasion Society."

My palms grew clammy, and I wiped them discreetly on my jeans, hoping no one would notice my sudden case of the jitters. "Ah, hi. I'm Paris, and these are the other book club members."

He waved at the group. "If you don't already know me, I'm Dax Granger."

Everyone introduced themselves, then nibbled on a pastry or sipped their coffee.

As I scrambled to collect the scattered bookmarks, Dax surprised me by crouching to help. The whiff of his cologne, sandalwood and musk, tickled my senses. Reaching for the same bookmark, his fingers grazed mine. I jerked my hand back, my face flushing.

"Thanks," I mumbled, avoiding eye contact.

"No problem. Always happy to lend a hand, especially to a damsel in distress."

"Well, I wouldn't say *distress*, more like momentarily flustered by flying bookmarks."

Trying to back away from him, I stumbled over my own feet, nearly crashing into a display of small town romances. Silently cursing my inability to act like a normal human being around this man, I let out a nervous laugh.

*Oh, for Austen's sake!* Did he think I was a complete dork? Or worse, did he pity me for being so obviously awkward? And why did I care?

Plopping onto my chair, I gave Dax a sideways look. His appearance was marked by a chiseled jawline softened by a light layer of scruff. His hazel eyes were set beneath short, tousled light-brown hair—*and* talk about broad shoulders, his clothing did little to hide the muscles beneath. Classic dark-wash jeans hugged his legs, ending in sturdy leather boots.

"Let me guess..." Aunt Margo eyed Dax with the precision of a hawk spotting a field mouse. "You must be a Scorpio."

"Close." He sat in the chair beside mine. "Sagittarius."

"Ah, yes, like I said, a Sagittarius." My aunt sat up. "That would explain the athletic physique, and I'm betting a thirst for adventure. You archers love to experience new things." She tapped her chin before turning to me. "Whereas Virgos like Paris prefer immersing themselves in routines." My aunt peered at me and slowly grinned. "Why stay inside organizing your meticulously color-coded underwear drawer when a handsome Sag like Dax here promises a hunky distraction?"

*Oh, Aunt Margo.* My cheeks burned. Though I didn't believe in astrology, Aunt Margo certainly knew how to embarrass me while having a bit of fun at Dax's expense.

"Well, you know us Virgos." I flicked my wrist dismissively. "Constantly analyzing and overthinking. It's a wonder we ever leave the house."

Dax faced the others. "I appreciate you letting me crash your book club today. Samuel thinks I need to expand my reading preferences."

He was definitely not the type to appreciate the finer points of a quiet, book-filled lifestyle. He was more likely to use a romance novel as a coaster for his beer than actually read it.

I frowned at Dax. "You do realize this book club mainly focuses on romance?"

Dax cracked his knuckles. "Well, I'm always open to trying new things. And I have read *Pride and Prejudice and Poltergeists*."

Everyone laughed.

"Dax, my friend, that's a masterpiece of literary mashups," Samuel said.

That settled it. Dax would never take this seriously or fit in with the Literary Persuasion Society, a group full of genuine bibliophiles. It wasn't that I didn't think he could appreciate a good romance novel—okay, maybe it was a little bit of that. Mostly, it was the way he disrupted the comfortable routine I'd come to rely on with my friends.

The book club was my safe space, a place where I could be myself and have discussions with like-minded people. Dax threatened to upend that delicate balance. Maybe it was unfair to judge him so quickly, but the thought of change, of letting someone new into our little literary bubble, made my chest tighten.

Perhaps it was time to put him to the test and hope he'd leave without a fuss.

Snatching a random paperback off a table, I gestured at the book. "Have you ever even read a romance, Dax?"

He shifted in his seat. "Can't say that I have. I don't read much outside of horror."

"A popular genre, but where's the sentiment? The intimate connections?" I asked.

"Oh, you might be surprised." A thoughtful expression crossed his face. "Horror can delve into some pretty deep themes about the human condition, and the characters often have to rely on each other to survive. That can lead to some intense emotional bonds. And while I'm admittedly more of an adrenaline junkie when it comes to my reading preferences, I can appreciate the appeal of a good love story, as long as it's a subplot."

My foot tapped. "I'll take swoon-worthy over scary any day. Romance challenges us to open our hearts, to be vulnerable."

Carmen stood and excused herself to the bathroom. Rachel's phone rang and she stepped outside to take the call.

Dax held up one of my bookmarks featuring a couple in a passionate embrace. "You are aware that it's all fantasy, right?"

"Oh, and I suppose your thrillers and horror novels are the epitome of realism?" I pushed hair out of my face. "Romance is about the human experience, the depth of emotions, and the transformative power of love. There's beauty and truth in that, even if the stories are sometimes idealized."

"More like the power of cheesy lines and predictable plots." He leaned in closer, his voice lowering. "A good thriller keeps you on the edge of your seat, heart pounding, palms sweating. Now that's a good read."

How dare he disparage my favorite genre in my own shop!

Clasping my hands tightly on my lap, I frowned. "Face it, Dax. You're too scared to embrace the emotional roller-coaster that is a well-written romance."

He laughed. "Scared? *Nah.* I just prefer to keep my adrenaline pumping with a good old-fashioned horror or thriller."

My scowl wavered at his stubborn refusal to see the light. There was something undeniably attractive about a man who stood his ground, even if he was completely misguided in his literary preferences.

Aunt Margo clucked her tongue. "Now, now, you two. There's room for all kinds of books in this world. Why don't we focus on our love of reading instead of bickering like an old married couple?"

Samuel clapped his hands. "That's what we're here for. Lively debates on books, genres, and the existential dread of running out of coffee."

"Or the eternal question of whether kale belongs on pizza," Aunt Margo said.

Dax's crooked grin returned full force. "Why do I get the feeling that you're not exactly thrilled with me being here, Paris?"

I sucked in a breath, then exhaled. While this man was the epitome of everything I wasn't—more brawn than Byron, more deadlifts than Dostoevsky—it was the thought of letting someone new in, of opening myself up to the possibility of disruption and uncertainty, that made my hackles rise.

*Channel your inner Emma Woodhouse.*

"I apologize if I was rude. I'm just excited to share the joy of romance novels with a new reader. There's something magical about the way these stories can transport you to another world, make you feel all the feels, and leave you with a sense of hope and happiness. It's like a warm hug for your soul. And don't even get me started on the swoony heroes and the fierce heroines who..." My voice trailed off, realizing I was rambling. "See for yourself." I tossed the book to him, half-expecting him to fumble the catch. But of course, with his annoyingly perfect reflexes, he snatched it out of the air with ease.

"*Heartstrings and Handcuffs?*" He studied the cover, his eyebrows raising. "Sounds...intriguing."

Why did I have to pick a book with such a suggestive

title? My face was probably the same shade as the cerise wallpaper.

"It's not what you think," I mumbled, suddenly fascinated by a loose thread on my tee. "It's a metaphor. For, you know, the ups and downs of relationships."

Dax placed the book back on the table. "I'm sure it's a great read."

Samuel and Aunt Margo were staring at us. I squirmed in my seat.

Samuel clapped Dax on the shoulder. "Don't mind Paris. She's just protective of her bookish sanctuary. We're happy to have you, and I'm sure you'll bring a unique viewpoint to our discussions."

Returning, Carmen smiled warmly at Dax. "Oh, yes. We're pleased to have you join our literary group. Fresh meat—I mean, fresh perspectives—are always welcome."

"Yes, the more the merrier!" Aunt Margo said. "A strapping young stud like yourself might just be the pizzazz we need in our book club."

Dax flashed a grin that could have melted butter. "Well, I'm flattered by the warm greeting. And glad to be here."

My foot twitched against the chair leg, but I kept my face expressionless. No need to get myself worked up. He wouldn't be here long. Dax wasn't one of us and he'd realize that soon enough.

Clearing my throat, I tried to regain control of the situation. "Yes, well, as much as we all love a good meet-cute, perhaps we should actually discuss the book? That is the purpose of a book club, last time I checked."

Carmen waved off my attempt at literary reason. "We're just trying to make Dax feel like part of the gang. Isn't that what book clubs are all about? Bonding over our shared love of reading?"

I bit my tongue, knowing she had a point. It was just, well, something about Dax's presence that made me feel off-kilter, like a bookshelf teetering under the weight of too many books.

Staring at him, my eyes narrowed. What was this exercise junkie really doing here?

My defenses snapped back into place, but this time, it was more out of self-preservation than judgment.

What if Dax saw through my careful disguise and realized I was just a weird, insecure girl who didn't like strangers entering her world without an invite? What if he...if he judged *me* as harshly as I was judging him?

None of that mattered because he didn't belong. This was a bookshop and a book club that catered to romance readers. While on occasion I did order other genres for my customers, I couldn't quite picture Dax reading a steamy bodice-ripper. Unless, of course, he was here to research the mating habits of the wild romance reader in their natural habitat. In which case, I hoped he brought a notebook and a healthy sense of humor because things were about to get delightfully awkward.

But...he was kinda cute. I started picturing those muscular arms reshelving books...

*Oh, for the love of Austen!* This was not the time to ogle a temporary club member.

In the small town universe I inhabited, where the highlight of any social gathering was discussing the latest scandal over potluck dinners (and let me tell you, Mrs. Jenkins' affair with the mailman was the talk of the town), men like Dax were anomalies—rare comets streaking across a starlit sky. I could admire the spectacle but keep my distance, knowing full well the burn of getting too close.

# Chapter Three

THE BOOK CLUB MEMBERS CHATTED WITH DAX like he was a celebrity guest on a reality TV show about book lovers.

Rachel returned and sat beside me. She pulled more goodies from her purse—a plastic bag packed with her infamous snickerdoodle cookies, and the aroma of cinnamon and vanilla wafted through the air.

"All right everyone, let's dive into this month's pick: *Nautical Nuptials*." I clasped my hands. "I must say, Captain Thorne's brooding intensity had me at *Ahoy*."

Carmen lifted her brows. "Brooding? More like emotionally unavailable."

"But emotionally *available* men don't make for enthralling page-turners." Aunt Margo's turquoise bracelets jingled when she lifted the paperback. "His character just needed the right woman to traverse his waters."

"Which is exactly why I adore romance," I said. "It's about finding someone who compliments you both body and soul, not just fitting some formulaic mold."

Dax snorted. "Give me a thriller or horror story any day of the week—something that gets your heart pumping."

Not this again. A twinge of defensiveness struck my chest. It was as if he had just dismissed an entire genre—and by extension, a part of me—with a flippant wave of his hand.

"Oh, *pish posh!* There's nothing wrong with a little escapism, young man. It spices things up if you know what I mean." Aunt Margo looked at Dax, and he let out a surprised chuckle.

"Well, there's more to romance than just the stereo-typical bodice-rippers," I said, my tone softening. "There are quite a few genres that blend romance with other themes. Like Gothic romance, for example. It combines the suspense and thrills of horror with the emotional depth and character development of romance. Or so I've heard, I haven't read much of it myself. And really, when you think about it, a lot of genres can have romantic elements. Suspense, fantasy, even sci-fi. It's all about the storytelling and how the author brings the characters to life."

Dax raised an eyebrow. "*Huh*. Guess I always assumed romance was just, you know, all about the mushy stuff."

I grabbed one of Rachel's cookies. "Oh, there's defi-nitely mushy stuff. There's also adventure, mystery, and sometimes even danger. It's a lot more diverse than people give it credit for. You should read one sometime."

Dax sat back, crossing his arms over his chest in a way that emphasized his biceps. It was like he was flexing without meaning to—or was he? Hard to tell with someone like him. Even though I could appreciate the view, I couldn't decide whether to be annoyed or intrigued by his mere presence.

Dax shook his head. "No thanks. Romance is not for me. It's just a bunch of unrealistic fairy tales."

Rachel scoffed. "And horror isn't? Don't even get me started on the plot holes. Like anyone could survive half the stuff that happens in horror novels or movies. "

Samuel nodded. "True, and a lot of romance stories rely on tired old tropes. But the best ones have complex characters, genuine emotions, and relationships that feel earned. When it's done well, Dax, romance can be just as compelling and insightful about the human condition as any other genre."

Dax let out a short laugh. "I doubt it. How about the romance cliché of misunderstandings and cheesy declarations of undying devotion? How original."

"As if a masked killer chasing scantily-clad coeds is the height of creativity." This guy was infuriating. Cute, but infuriating. "Forget it. Clearly, you're not open to other genres."

"And you're not open to admitting that romance is just formulaic fluff," he countered.

We glared at each other for a moment, the friction rising between us. I had to admit, there was something fun about arguing with someone who was so passionate about their opinions, even if they were dead wrong.

But I wasn't about to let him win this one. "You know what, Dax? I think you're just scared."

He blinked. "Scared? Of what?"

"Of admitting that deep down, underneath all that macho posturing, you might just enjoy a love story."

Dax's jaw dropped. "I...*what?* No. Absolutely not."

I grinned. "Methinks the lady doth protest too much."

He shook his head, his lips twitching. "You're cute, you know that?"

Rachel closed her bag of cookies. "If you two are done flirting, can we get back to the book club meeting now?"

Fire swept over my skin and I fought the urge to face my face. "We were *not* flirting," I looked at Dax. "If you're that narrowminded, than by all means, keep reading your genre and leave us to ours."

Dax lifted his brow. "Better than reading about shirtless pirates."

Aunt Margo scoffed. "Oh, don't be such a spoilsport, Dax. Scantily clad bandits can be very enlightening."

Carmen laughed. "Margo, I think you just enjoy the, *ahem*—treasure chests."

Samuel snickered. "Whatever floats your boat—or pirate ship."

Everyone laughed, then they started debating the book's love interests.

*Dax Granger didn't belong.* I kept repeating it like a mantra. Then I caught him staring at me with a crooked smile and my brain short-circuited, leaving me fumbling for words and praying I didn't have coffee breath.

*Ugh.* Dax was here, for better or worse, and I guess I needed to find a way to deal with it.

Dax leaned closer to me. "I like your hair. It's pretty."

He gave me this smoldering look—the kind that could make a girl forget the difference between Austen's prose and a heart monitor's beeps.

Okay, sure, it might be tempting to get swept up in the excitement of something new and shiny. But I knew better than to fall for a handsome face and a set of abs that could make a Greek god weep with envy. I was a woman of substance, a connoisseur of the written word. I couldn't be swayed by a charming smile and flirty compliments.

I ruthlessly brushed cookie crumbs from my shirt and

joined in on the discussion. "And beyond the lusty sere-nades by the captain, let's not dismiss the complexities of relationships, the joys and pains of love." I glanced at Dax. "You can't find that theme in any horror novel."

"How do you know if you've never read one?" Dax tilted his head. "Sometimes it's the dark that makes us reach for the light."

I had to glance away from his infuriatingly charming face. How did someone manage to be so annoying yet so...visually pleasing?

In books, these encounters were always fraught with romantic tension, the prelude to an inevitable passionate entanglement. Except this was real life, where a bookish girl like me didn't befriend a beefcake like him.

He didn't fit into *my* world. We were complete oppo-sites. I suppose his perfect jawline and wavy, light-brown hair could have given any Harlequin model a run for their money, but he was too...polished, like those pretty boys who spent more time in front of a mirror than in a book-store. And the guy thrived on horror. Me? I'd rather curl up with romance any day of the week.

I flashed him a tight-lipped smile, hoping it conveyed both politeness and dismissal. "Thanks for sharing your opinions, Dax. Now, who wants to discuss chapter five?"

"Wait...I've got an idea." Dax straightened, his biceps bulging in a distracting way. "How about a reading chal-lenge, Paris? We could do a genre swap. You read two of my favorite horror novels, and I'll read these...voyages of love."

"What a delightful notion! Paris, honey, it might do you good to step away from your reading routine," Aunt Margo said. "You might discover a new genre... or perhaps a new perspective on life and love."

Samuel patted Dax's knee. "And Dax, my friend, a little

romance never hurt anyone. I quite enjoy reading it myself. In fact, I wager you'll be quoting Shakespearean sonnets in a graveyard in no time!"

Dax laughed. "We'll see about that, Samuel. I'm not sure I have the dramatic flair to pull off a graveyard sonnet recital."

"Oh, I don't know," I teased. "I can totally picture you, perched atop a tombstone, proclaiming, *'But soft, what light through yonder window breaks?'*"

The image of Dax dramatically reciting limericks among headstones caused a round of laughter. Dax's eyes crinkled, genuine amusement softening his features.

"Horror novels are like a mental workout. They keep you up late, get your heart racing. Trust me, it's a rush," Dax said.

"But seriously. Thanks, but no thanks," I said firmly. "My appreciation of an adrenaline rush is a last-minute book sale, not a ghostly tale."

"Oh, don't be such a book snob, Paris," Rachel said.

I narrowed my eyes. I couldn't believe what I was hearing. It was like my own book club had turned against me, throwing me to the literary wolves—or in this case, the horror-loving gym rat.

As I looked around at the eager faces of my friends, I realized that I was outnumbered. They seemed genuinely excited about the idea of a genre swap.

"Glad the group agrees." Dax grinned at everyone, as if he'd been born to charm the socks off of unsuspecting book clubbers. "What's the worst that could happen? You might actually enjoy a different genre."

I hesitated, considering his proposal, then offered Dax a small, apologetic smile. "It's not that I'm allergic to trying new things," I said, choosing my words carefully. "I'm just uneasy about reading books that aren't my literary jam. Romance novels have been my go-to for so long."

Sushi appeared and gave Dax's shoes a few delicate sniffs. Dax made the risky move of offering his hand to the furry critic. After another sniff, Sushi rubbed her side against his leg, fur collecting in drifts across his jeans.

Should I offer him a lint roller? Probably. Yet for some inexplicable reason, I remained comfortably planted in my seat, refusing to lift a finger.

If Sushi wanted to fraternize with the enemy, who was I to stand in the way of her newfound allegiance? I'd just sit back and watch as my cat shamelessly sought attention from the man who had so impolitely interrupted our peaceful book club meeting.

Samuel pointed at my cat. "See? Even Sushi thinks it's a splendid idea."

I shook my head. "Her judgment is questionable at best. She also thinks chasing dust bunnies is a sport."

"Oh, come on, Paris. It might be fun," Dax said.

"Paris, *querida*," Carmen cooed from where she sat. "It could be an illuminating experience."

"Think about it. This reading challenge might just liven up your bookstagram content, too," Rachel said.

I squirmed in my seat under the weight of their collective stares. For a moment, I felt like a kid who'd stumbled into the wrong birthday party—surrounded by gleeful faces and inside jokes I couldn't quite grasp. It was as if they were all in on some secret I had yet to uncover, and I was an outsider looking in.

Dax leaned forward, his elbows resting on his knees. "I dare you, bookworm."

Maybe I was being too harsh. I realized I was guilty of the same narrow-mindedness I'd accused Dax of. I was a bookshop owner, and shouldn't let myself be such a book snob. Sure, Dax and I couldn't be more different. He probably considered trail mix the fifth essential food group and had never been slain by a fictional character's death. Cats, coffee, and pastries were the holy trinity of my existence, while he undoubtedly worshiped dumbbells, veggie powders, and curated workout playlists.

That didn't mean I couldn't be civil. And this was my bookshop, my book club, and I wasn't about to let some muscle-bound Adonis throw me off my game. Even if his spicy cologne did make my knees feel a little weak.

Then, something clicked in my brain—a lightbulb moment, if you will. I couldn't let him get to me.

I'd faced far greater challenges than a few goosebump-inducing novels—like that time I had to rescue Mrs. Fitzpatrick's pet rat from the top shelf of the sci-fi romance section before Sushi could pounce—a true test of my patience and agility.

If I could make Dax eat his words (and perhaps a slice of humble pie) in the process? Well, that would just be the cherry on top of this delightfully bookish debate.

"You're right, there's always room for growth and discovery." I sighed. "How about we start small? I'll give your horror recommendations a chance, but something on the milder side to ease me into it. And in return, I'll pick out a romance novel that I think might appeal to your tastes."

No way could he get through the first few pages of the story I had in mind, much less the first chapter. This would all be over, he'd quit the book club, and my life could return to its quiet order.

He held out his hand, grinning. "I can work with that, and we might just find some common ground after all."

I shook his hand, his grip warm and firm. The flutter in my stomach and the tingling in my fingertips were simply a result of the anticipation of the genre swap, and not any sort of chemistry or attraction to Dax. He was a wild card, a plot twist I hadn't seen coming.

And as much as I hated to admit it, that scared me. I was used to changes happening between the pages of a book, not in my own life.

"To be clear, I'm only doing this to prove romances are superior reads."

"Of course. Let the genre-defying challenge begin!" Dax replied, a triumphant edge to his voice.

# Chapter Four

*Dax*-

AFTER FINISHING MY EARLY MORNING TRAINING session, I hit the streets of downtown, the sun just beginning to flex its muscles and warm the air. The area was already buzzing, a hive of activity that matched my own energy. The smell of black coffee from a nearby cafe cut through the spring air, sharp and invigorating

Perfect. Just like the precise form I demanded from my clients during a deadlift.

My trip to the health store had left me disappointed—they were out of the detox juice cleanse I swore by for my post-workout recovery, so I'd have to snag it online now instead.

"Morning, Dax!" Samuel waved from across the street.

"Samuel. How's it going?" I made my way over, my boots smacking the concrete.

"Hard to have complaints when the weather's this generous." He pushed up his glasses. "That reading challenge you cooked up—swapping genres with Paris—is a bold move, my friend."

"Not gonna lie, I'm pumped for the dare." My attempt to keep a straight face failed, a real smile breaking through at the thought of spending time with Paris. "And if this is what it takes to get Paris hooked on horror, consider me ready."

"And you'll really read a romance or two?"

"Of course. There's no backing down in the gym and the same goes here."

Samuel clapped me on the back. "You've got guts, Dax. I've got to say, I don't shy away from a romance novel when it's the club's pick. And I applaud your strategy. It's definitely...*inventive*." His expression gleamed with shrewdness, and I knew he saw right through me.

"Strategy?" I cleared my throat, feigning ignorance. "The swap is all in the spirit of broadening our horizons. Purely bookish pursuits."

"Uh-huh. Whatever you say." Samuel glanced toward the sky where a kite floated lazily, its ribbon tail tangling with the branches of an oak.

"Well, yeah. The genre swap is an experiment. Like a new training session to build up the muscle of the mind."

"So you say, yet I can't help wondering if you have alternative motives for joining the book club." His voice lowered as if someone might overhear us. "Instead of going through all this subterfuge, have you considered just asking Paris out on a proper date?"

The way my heart kicked against my ribcage was downright mutinous like I'd just finished a triathlon. The mere thought of dating Paris, of sitting across from her at a candlelit table sent an electric jolt through my veins, igniting a fire I'd been suppressing for far too long.

Yeah, joining the book club was a ploy to get her attention.

What had caught my interest wasn't Paris's skill at running her own bookshop or her dedicated bookstagram feed, but the strength and independence she showed. In a world where physical strength was my domain, it was her mental fortitude and steadfast commitment to doing things her own way that stood out to me. She was unlike anyone else in town, which positively made an impression. Plus, she was hot.

Shifting my weight from one foot to the other, I looked away. "I don't know what you're talking about."

"Come now. You've got a soft spot for her, don't you? You're a man of depth—attentive, engaging, and you're willing to go the extra mile for someone you care about."

I sighed, resignation threading through my voice. "There's definitely something about her that's got me hooked. But she seems to prefer those overly romantic dudes, knights on horseback declaring their love in verse. And I'm not *that* guy."

Samuel chuckled. "Dax, my boy, Paris is special, yes. She doesn't date often, and I think it's because she's waiting for someone who can match her wit and uniqueness. And between you and me, I think you fit the bill better than any Byron-quoting equestrian."

"Is that right?" The question popped out before I could stop it, and my skepticism must've been painted on my face because Samuel grinned wider.

"Believe in yourself! You've got more to offer than you think."

I rubbed the back of my neck. "I don't know..."

Samuel slapped me on the shoulder. "Paris appreciates authenticity, and that's you, my friend. Be brave!"

It was a cruel twist of fate to be smitten with a woman who likely saw me as nothing more than just another local guy, a gym rat. Yet I was a grown man of thirty-five, reduced to a bundle of nerves at the prospect of asking Paris out. The irony was not lost on me—a man who prided himself on his discipline and control, now struggling with an all-consuming infatuation.

I'd always believed in the power of mind over matter, in the ability to sculpt not only the body but also the spirit through sheer force of will. I'd spent countless hours in the gym, honing my physique and coaching others to do the same, preaching the gospel of clean living and mental fortitude. Yet, when it came to Paris, all my carefully cultivated self-mastery evaporated in her presence.

"Guess you have a point..." My gaze focused on Prose & Positivity further down the street. "If I can face down a grueling workout routine, I should be able to handle real-life relationships...right?"

"Right. So, when are you planning to make your move?"

"Let's not get ahead of ourselves." Although a plan was already forming in my mind. "During the genre swap, I wanna get to know her better."

Samuel bobbed his head. "Well, my friend, I wish you the best of luck. Because I have a feeling you two might just be the perfect match." He glanced at his wristwatch and let out a low whistle. "Oh, would you look at the time! I better get going if I want to squeeze in a round of golf before I meet my next client."

"Enjoy your game, Samuel. And thanks for the pep-talk." I smiled, genuinely grateful for his support.

With a final wave, Samuel ambled off towards his car parked at the curb.

Samuel was right—I had to believe in myself if I wanted to win Paris's heart. She might be out of my league, but I had to at least try. After all, isn't that what the characters in my favorite novels always did? They slayed monsters and conquered their fears.

Strolling along the sidewalk, I spotted Paris outside her pink bookshop—my heart performing an acrobatic stunt at the sight of her. Ironic, considering I had just been wrestling with the idea of her ever considering me as more than just a friend.

Approaching her I aimed for nonchalance, hoping to mask the fact that I'd been thinking about her nonstop since the book club meeting. I halted near her on the sidewalk.

"Hey, Paris. Fancy meeting you here. It's almost like you work here or something."

She looked up from her phone, startled, and it took a moment for recognition to dawn in those mesmerizing blue eyes of hers. And when it did, a slow grin spread across her face—the kind of smile that could make even the grumpiest of nonreaders crack a spine.

"Hey, Dax." She shifted the phone to her other hand. "I was just considering shots for my Instagram account. Trying to capture the essence of my bibliophile kingdom in a single frame."

"How about posing with a new romance release? Or a cute shot of you reading to your feline overlord?"

Even though romance wasn't my normal genre, I found myself wanting to know more about the stories that captured her heart. And I couldn't resist the opportunity to tease her about her adorable cat.

"Great ideas and I have taken similar pics..." She

launched into a description of her other posts, her expression shiny with passion.

The way she spoke about books—like they were precious gifts waiting to be discovered—made me see them in a whole new light. It was like she had the power to make even the most mundane things seem captivating.

"Are you ready for your first horror read?" I wore a sly grin. "Because I have the perfect book for you. It's guaranteed to make you sleep with the lights on for a week, bookworm."

Paris wrinkled her nose, looking about as thrilled as a vegan at a steakhouse. "I don't know about this...I'm having second thoughts, Dax. I prefer my scares to be limited to the occasional paper cut or coffee stain on a first edition."

"Come on, you promised you'd give it a shot. And I'm holding up my end of the bargain by reading a romance. I'm ready to defy my own preconceptions. I know romance isn't my usual genre, but that doesn't mean I won't give it a go."

She shook her head, throwing her hands up. "I suppose it's too late to back out now."

"I bet you'll be a horror convert by the time you're done. You'll be trading in your bookmarks for a nightlight and a teddy bear."

Paris rolled her eyes. "Don't count on it. I'm made of sterner stuff than that. Although I'll admit, I'm curious to see what dark and twisty tales you recommend."

"Trust me, Paris. By the time we're done with this experiment, you'll be seeing thrillers and *me* in a whole new light."

She turned her attention back to her phone, fiddling with the settings. Her lips twitched. "Like the fact that you know how to read something other than gym equipment manuals?"

Staggering back a step, I clutched my chest at her teasing. "*Ouch*. You wound me. I'll have you know that I'm a man of many talents. Reading just happens to be one of them."

She laughed, a sound that was quickly becoming one of my favorite things in the world. "All right, all right. I suppose I can give horror a chance."

"And if you find yourself swooning over the brooding, misunderstood monster, I promise not to say I told you so."

Paris scoffed, crossing her arms over her chest. "*Please*. I have standards, you know. I don't fall for every creature of the night with a tragic backstory."

It was like we were engaged in a game of verbal chess, each move carefully calculated to keep the other on their toes.

Leaning in closer, I lowered my voice. "Ah, but what about a dashing, book-loving personal trainer with a heart of gold?"

A faint blush colored her cheeks. "Nice try, Casanova. I think I'll stick to my fictional heroes for now. Less chance of disappointment that way."

A frown pulled at my lips Okay...what did she mean by that? Was it just a playful jab, or did her comment hint at a deeper wound? I made a mental note to tread carefully, to earn her trust before attempting to scale the walls she'd obviously erected around herself.

"You know, I'm glad we're doing this." I rubbed my chin. "And I'm thinking we should take it one step further. Really immerse ourselves in the world of each storyline."

Her brows puckered. "What do you mean?"

"After we read each book, we go on an outing related to

the story to get the full experience. Like if the romance novel takes place at a fancy ball, we go dancing. Or if my story is set in a haunted mansion, we visit a spooky old house. It's like bringing the books to life. We'll be like the main characters, living out the story in real time."

"Um, yeah, I guess that might be kinda fun." Paris checked her phone screen and started texting someone.

Rocking on my heels, I watched her. Damn. I was utterly captivated by the woman standing before me. In a town where conformity was the norm, where people clung to the familiar like a well-worn security blanket, Paris was a vibrant anomaly. While others might have scoffed at her quirky style and bookish ways, I found them endearing. It was clear Paris wasn't interested in fitting into anyone's mold. She was unapologetically herself, and that was a rare and beautiful thing.

"I like that you're not like anyone else in this town."

She looked up and lowered her phone. "I suppose life would be rather dull if we were all predictable."

My gaze held hers. "And you, Paris Novak, are anything but dull."

"Is that a good thing or a bad thing?"

I grinned. "It's a great freaking thing. You're unique. Exceptional. Don't ever let anyone tell you otherwise."

"You really mean that?" she asked, tilting her head. "Quirkiness and all?"

"Definitely. In fact, I like you just the way you are, Paris."

Her eyebrows shot up, mouth open as if she wasn't used to receiving straightforward compliments. Then a slow, genuine smile spread across her face, lighting up her features in a way that made my heart stutter.

"I appreciate that, Dax. It...means a lot."

Standing there on the sun-dappled streets of Bluebell Bend with the woman of my dreams, I made a vow to myself. I would do whatever it took to win Paris's heart—even if it meant a departure from my horror reads and diving headfirst into romance.

After all, if there was one thing I'd learned from my favorite stories, it was that sometimes the greatest risks yielded the greatest rewards. And Paris Novak? She was a reward worth fighting for.

# Chapter Five

THE PERFUME OF FRESH LILACS AND SUN-WARMED grass wafted through the open windows of Prose & Positivity. I closed the bookshop and indulged in a little 'me time' in the reading nook, sipping on lavender-honey iced tea and munching on a savory Caprese sandwich.

The reading nook, a snug little alcove, was my favorite spot in the bookshop. With its overstuffed armchairs, fluffy throw pillows, and the vintage coffee table, it was a secret hideaway where my customers or I could lose ourselves in a good book.

It was in this very nook I often found myself reflecting on my life. Which up until now had been a blend of romance novels, bad first dates, and cat hair, and trust me, all of which stick to you in unexpected ways.

Now, in a shocking twist, I was in uncharted territory—reading a horror novel. It was as if I'd suddenly traded in my cozy blanket and fuzzy slippers for a flashlight and a sense of impending doom.

Closing the book, I sighed. "Is proving the superiority of romance really that important to me?"

"Meow." Sushi lounged in a soft, plush cat bed in the corner.

My gaze roamed the tidy rows of romance paperbacks, making me feel like a traitor.

"I'm reading horror," I grumbled, then turned to Sushi. "*Horror!*"

Sushi groomed her paw, apparently indifferent to my existential crisis.

I sighed again, realizing this reading competition with Dax was like trying to navigate a minefield on roller skates —scary and disorienting, with a high probability of falling flat on my face. But I was nothing if not determined (some might say stubborn, but I prefer the term 'tenacious'), and I refused to let a few scares keep me from proving my point.

If I could handle the daily drama of running a bookshop in a small town occupied by colorful characters and their equally colorful opinions, surely I could handle a few fictional frights.

Lifting the well-worn copy of *It's Alive!* by Merry Shaw that Dax had loaned me from his own collection, I settled in to read another chapter.

Over the last week, I'd been sneaking in chapters between customers, staying up late to read just one more page (which inevitably turned into ten), and even contemplating the Gothic narrative while sipping my morning coffee.

The Victorian gloom of Vincent's tale—a retired scientist turned hotelier with a flair for reanimation— was un-put-downable. I'd even started pondering the nature of humanity and the darkness that lurked in the corners of our souls...when I wasn't jumping at every creak of the floorboard.

With one hand, I stroked my cat's silky fur. "This book

isn't so bad. Sure, it's giving me enough goosebumps to last a lifetime, but it's entertaining."

Sushi flicked her ears in acknowledgment, yet remained noncommittal.

Maybe this was exactly what I needed. A chance to let go of my death grip on the familiar and embrace something new. Maybe I've been missing out all this time by only reading anything and everything romance-y.

I continued reading, my heart pounding during certain parts of the story, and at other times a tear came to my eye that I quickly swiped away. I couldn't let Sushi see me getting emotional. I'd never live it down.

When I finished the final pages of *It's Alive!*, I stretched and smiled.

"Oh, don't give me that look." I huffed. "I'm allowed to branch out, aren't I? Expand my literary horizons?"

Sushi just stared at me, then stretched and moseyed over to me. She proceeded to hop up onto my thighs and get comfortable.

I sat up, causing Sushi to wobble on my lap. "Still, this is a pretty big deal for me, actually enjoying a horror story."

*Oh, no.* This couldn't lead to anything good! What's next, taking up cross-fit? I grimaced at the image.

The bell above the door jingled, announcing the arrival of Dax, and Sushi hopped off my lap. My heart fluttered at the sight of him. Then I stiffened and cursed myself for the lusty reaction to the newest member of the book club.

Dax moseyed inside and towered over my chair as if a Greek god had descended from Mount Olympus, trading in his toga for a pair of well-worn jeans, a fitted shirt, and stylish boots. It was an infuriatingly attractive combination that had no business affecting me the way it did.

No business at all!

It wasn't just his good-looks that threw me off balance, though that certainly didn't help. I was used to my life being predictable, each day following a habitual pattern of reading and running the bookshop. Now with Dax around, I was reading horror (gasp!) —*yes, horror!*

No matter how many times I said it, it still sounded surreal.

He took a seat across from me. "I saw the lights on and thought I'd stop in. Ready to discuss your first foray into horror? Did you finish the book?"

"Yes, just now in fact."

"Did you like the story, bookworm?"

"Okay, so..." I focused on the leather-bound hardback in my hands. "It wasn't as bad as I thought it would be. Actually, it was really good." I rushed the last word out. It was hard enough admitting I'd liked the storyline, let alone confessing it to Dax of all people. I could practically feel his smug grin burning into me.

"Wait, hold up. Did I just hear the romance devotee admit to enjoying a horror novel?" Dax teased.

I rolled my eyes. "Just because I didn't hate one novel doesn't mean I'm ready to don a black cloak and start reciting Edgar Allan Poe."

Dax chuckled, leaning back in his chair. "At least you're appreciating the nuances of a good scare. And that's what I've been trying to tell you, horror isn't as one-dimensional as you think."

Shaking my head, I snorted. "I'm still very much a romance girl at heart. And I'll confess the book made me realize there's more to the genre than I supposed."

"Maybe there's hope for you yet, bookworm. Who knows, you might like the dark side..." Dax's gaze smoldered, and for a brief, heart-palpitating second, I swore a flicker of desire flared in his eyes.

I fumbled with the book in my lap, nearly sending it tumbling to the floor, before I reminded myself that flirting was simply part of his annoying charm.

Shifting in my seat, I quickly changed the subject. "And let's not forget about the romantic undertones in *It's Alive!*, the love and longing Vincent felt for Edwina was so beautiful and tragic."

"You and your fascination with romantic narratives..." Dax let out a modest chuckle. "Okay, fine, I'll give you that one."

With a cheeky grin, I gestured towards the shelves brimming with bodice-rippers and bare-chested male models. "What can I say? I'm a sucker for a schmaltzy love story, no matter the genre."

Dax shook his head. "Paris, you're comparing hot summer flings to chilling nightmares here. Horror and romance serve different purposes."

"I know, but that doesn't mean they can't coexist or even teach us something." Giving his leg a playful nudge with my foot, I wiggled my eyebrows. "I'll concede this round to your macabre perspective, but I'm not abandoning the crusade to prove romance reigns supreme."

"Wouldn't expect anything less from you." He winked, then stood up. "We should head out to our spooktacular field trip this evening. We can explore this abandoned hotel on the outskirts of town. And it perfectly complements the book."

We both went quiet. The air shifted, charged with something akin to static before a storm. All his ruggedness and bulging biceps, stark against the backdrop of pastel book spines and pink painted walls, seemed startlingly out of place.

Our differences were never so glaringly apparent. This man was dangerous. Insanely hot, but dangerous to my carefully controlled world.

And he kept disrupting the carefully crafted world I had built for myself. Dax represented change, a force that threatened to shake up my comfortable routine and push me out of my cozy, book-filled bubble.

What was next? Dragging me to the gym at ungodly hours? Or worse, what if he convinced me to enjoy it? I shuddered at the thought of trading in my cute cardigans for snug biker shorts.

Even as I tried to convince myself that Dax was nothing but trouble, I couldn't ignore the tiny part of me that was intrigued. What would it be like to take a chance on something unfamiliar?

I tilted my head. "Dax, I've gotta ask. What's with the horror fixation? You're not secretly planning to lure me into a hostel and sacrifice me to some ancient, eldritch god, are you?"

He let out a hearty laugh, the rumble charming and a little disconcerting. "No, no, nothing like that!" Dax waved a dismissive hand, the muscles in his forearms flexing in a way that momentarily distracted me. "It's just a passionate interest, I assure you. I promise I'm not hiding any cursed artifacts or voodoo dolls in my apartment."

I let out a sigh. "Well, that's a relief. So? Tell me why you like it so much."

Dax's voice took on a more serious tone. "Guess it goes back to when I was a teenager. Found this box of horror novels in my grandad's attic one summer. Those books were an escape from the everyday. You might not believe this, but

I used to get picked on a lot as a kid. I was scrawny and weak and an easy target for the bullies." His gaze turned distant as if visualizing those nights spent reading under the covers. "Horror showed me the resilience we're capable of. Like in the gym, when you're pushing your limits, it's not just about the physical. It's mental, too. Facing down something scary and coming out the other side...there's power in that."

My voice was soft, reflective. "That makes sense."

"Reading about ordinary people confronting their darkest fears, battling monsters, or surviving against all odds —it resonated with me. Made me realize there's something exhilarating about pushing through dread, about finding out what you're actually made of." Dax raked fingers through his hair. "Those nights, reading by flashlight, they changed me. It wasn't just about getting scared, it was learning that the genre speaks to the core of the human experience—the battle between light and darkness, good and evil, life and death."

So, it wasn't just a casual interest for Dax, horror was profoundly inspiring, and a symbol of the strength and perseverance inherent in us all, and all the while maintaining perfect hair and an impressive set of abs.

Or he just really enjoyed the adrenaline rush of being scared out of his well-defined muscles. Either way, I had to admire his love of reading and his willingness to embrace the edgier side of life—even if I still preferred my stories with a guaranteed happily ever after.

"I never thought of it that way."

"To me, horror and thrillers boil down to one thing— performance under pressure. It's what I live for, what I teach. There's no room for doubt in the gym, just like in life." He punched a fist into his open palm. "You set your goal, you chase it down, and you don't stop until you've crushed it."

I raised an eyebrow. "It sounds like those stories were more than just entertainment for you."

"They were. Plus, it's like hitting a new personal record at the gym. It's addictive." He jumped to his feet, his muscles rippling under his tight t-shirt, and jerked his head towards the door. "Let's go, bookworm."

My nerves did a jittery dance. I stay seated, setting the book on the table next to me. The only other time I'd dipped my toes into horror was when I'd watched that werewolf movie *Ginger Snacks*, and I spent a week giving the side-eye to every stray dog in the neighborhood. Now, having just read a dark gothic tale and Dax trying to coax me into an eerie night on the town, I could say goodbye to peaceful nights, and hello to an unhealthy obsession with checking under the bed.

Dax wagged a finger at me. "Hey, you agreed to this reading challenge, remember? And the outings that accompany each book."

Wandering around a derelict hotel? No thank you.

"Haunted places aren't exactly my idea of a good time."

His expression softened. "I promise, it's all in good fun. And if things get too intense, we can leave. I'll be right by your side the whole time. Please?"

Leaning back, I suddenly felt a slight kinship with him. Like me, Dax stood out like a sore thumb in our quaint little town, where everyone seemed to fit into neat, predictable boxes. Well, an insanely attractive, muscular thumb. And that's precisely what I was finding so refreshing about him. While I often felt like an outsider myself, Dax's brazen love for all things spooky made me realize I wasn't alone in my quirks. It was as if we were members of a secret club, where a passion for the unconventional was not only accepted but celebrated.

And if you're going to wander around a haunted location, you might as well do it with a cute guy by your side.

"Okay."

Channeling my inner Emma Woodhouse, I took a deep breath. I could do this. I could be witty, charming, and confident, even on a scary fieldtrip.

He held out his hand, and I hesitated before taking it. His grip was steady and tender, and I tried not to think about how perfectly our hands fit together.

"If I have nightmares, you'll owe me a lifetime supply of nightlights." I gave him a tentative smile.

What had I just agreed to?

I wasn't usually one for taking risks, preferring the safety and reliability of my books and my routines. Dax had a way of talking me into things that were outside of my comfort zone.

After I locked up the bookshop, we walked towards his car—a sleek black Dodge Charger parked at the curb. He opened the passenger door for me, and I slid onto the leather seat. Then almost got back out.

I liked Dax, he seemed like a nice enough guy, but I liked my life the way it was, and I didn't need him coming in and turning everything upside down with his persuasive smiles and flirtatiousness. I just had to get through this genre swap and get back to my life—the one rearranging my bookshelves to make room for more titles and tripping over my cat's extensive toy collection.

# Chapter Six

DAX DROVE THROUGH THE TOWN'S QUIET streets, the world beyond our windows slipping into soft focus like an old Hollywood film reel. Shadows, cast by a full moon, turned familiar landmarks into silhouettes as if our town had suddenly auditioned for a role in a low-budget horror flick. I half-expected to see a group of villagers with pitchforks and torches marching down Main Street, chanting ominously about the dangers of outsiders and the importance of maintaining small town traditions. But the only thing lurking in the gloom was Mrs. Henderson's Siamese cat, who seemed more interested in chasing moths than joining any sort of town uprising.

I elbowed him on the bicep. "Are you sure this hotel is haunted?"

Dax lifted his right hand. "Scout's honor. You'll see for yourself once we get there. Heritage House is located on the outskirts of town and hasn't been in business since the 1940s."

The car crept to a stop in front of Heritage House, its headlights briefly catching the tangled ivy smothering its

Victorian façade and overgrown gardens. The hotel stood as if plucked from the pages of a Gothic novel, with its ostentatious turrets and gables.

Sending a discreet text to Aunt Margo and Rachel, I informed them of my trip to an abandoned hotel with Dax. Just in case his love for horror turned out to be more Norman Bates than *Casper, the Friendly Ghost*, at least someone would know where to look for my remains.

Dax got out, his figure momentarily merging with the darkness before he came around to open my door. He offered me his arm with a lopsided grin and I linked my arm with his. We walked up to the hotel entrance, and Dax pulled open the heavy wooden door, revealing a candlelit cobwebbed foyer.

I glanced at him questioningly.

"Thought it'd be more atmospheric if we used candles," he said, shrugging. "I came by earlier to set it all up. I managed to pull some strings with one of my clients, the guy who owns this place. He's cool with us checking it out before he brings in the wrecking crew to flatten it and turn it into a park. Gotta love those connections, right?" Dax flashed a confident grin.

"The candles do set the mood, and this place isn't as creepy as I thought it would be. It's actually kinda cool and interesting."

We stepped over the threshold into a massive room with a front desk and seating, the once-lavish décor now dusty and faded. The air was thick with the musty scent of history, the kind that clings to old buildings. The chandelier, dulled by years of neglect, hung solemnly from the ceiling, its crystals catching the faint light and forming eerie reflections on the walls. We passed a grand staircase leading to upper-floors.

"Heritage House has a lot of history. For instance," Dax said, his voice taking on a theatrical tone, "the original owner of this hotel still wanders the halls. They say he's searching for someone."

"And what is this spectral proprietor looking for?"

"His lost love, of course."

I smiled and it calmed the slight jitters. "Ah, so even ghosts aren't immune to the allure of romance."

He chuckled. "Afraid not."

Dax and I wandered about, the floorboards creaking in the vast, empty space.

He escorted me past the stairs, removing a small flashlight from his coat pocket and flicking it on. "They say he can be heard on nights just like this one, wailing for his beloved, and those who hear his cries are cursed to—"

"Let me guess. Forever crave chocolate croissants at midnight? Because in that case, I might stick around. A little supernatural pastry addiction never hurt anyone."

Dax laughed. "I was gonna say 'be haunted by bad luck,' but your version's better."

"Of course it is," I teased.

The way he smiled at me caused my heart to do a backflip. Then my chest squeezed. No way could I let myself get swept up in the moment, no matter how charismatic he was.

Because the memory of Julian's betrayal still haunted me, making me feel insecure and scared whenever I interacted with guys. It was like this bitter aftertaste that just wouldn't go away, no matter how much time passed. Thinking about it made me feel sick to my stomach, like my insides were tying themselves into knots that might never come undone. The heart wounds had scabbed over, but even the slightest prod could rip them open again, unleashing all that pain and doubt. I had to keep Dax at a distance.

"Let's go this way." Dax motioned toward a shadowy corridor branching off from the main hall.

Meandering through the dimly lit passageways, our footsteps were muffled by the age-worn carpet, which had seen more wear and tear than a well-loved teddy bear. I had to admit there was a major creep-factor to this place and I stayed close to Dax, appreciating his protective vibe. Peeling wallpaper clung to the walls, patterns faded yet hinting at past grandeur, like a once-glamorous starlet who had traded in her sequins for a fluffy bathrobe and fuzzy slippers.

I peered inside a bedroom at dusty furniture, draped in tattered cloth. A chill draft swept through the corridor decorated with grandiose mirrors, their surfaces clouded with age. I shuddered and rubbed my arms.

"You cold?" Dax shrugged off his coat and handed it to me.

It was five sizes too big, but I slipped it on and his masculine cologne enveloped me, a heady fusion of citrusy notes and spicy, woody undertones. "Thanks."

We continued exploring, our conversation echoing through the halls. The flashlight's beam, shining on the walls painted us in a peek-a-boo of shadows and light.

Glancing at him, I could help thinking again about how different we were. His idea of a good time involved inspecting haunted locales and watching slasher flicks, while mine leaned more towards cozy bookstores and sappy Hallmark movies, but at the end of the day, we were both misfits in our own charming ways. Maybe this shared appreciation for the unusual would be the foundation for a beautiful, albeit somewhat peculiar, friendship.

He bumped my arm with his. "If this were a movie, this

is the part where the rugged hero stumbles upon a secret passage behind a bookshelf."

"Reality is rarely so convenient or cliché."

"Ah, but that's the thing about fiction...no limits," he said, his voice deepening to a quiet rumble. "In those love stories of yours, would the hero have the guts to go in for a kiss, risking the knockback?"

Before I could respond Dax's hand touched my arm and I froze, his touch electrifying my skin even through the cotton of his zip-up hoodie. He leaned in closer, his lips mere inches from mine. The air between us sizzled with heat and the intensity in his stare had a magnetic pull. His hand lowered, his thumb lightly caressing the curve of my bottom lip, and I nearly melted into a puddle of mushy girl gooeyness.

Moving my trembling hands to his shoulders, I tried to steady myself before my knees gave out. His chest rose and fell unsteadily, and then it hit me like a hardcover to the head—he was just as caught up in the moment as I was.

All I could focus on was the delicious heat of his body, the teasing brush of his fingertips on my flushed skin, and the way my heart threatened to pound right out of my chest. My eyes fluttered closed and I waited for his lips to touch mine. He lowered his head slowly, his minty breath fanning across my parted lips.

A sudden crash thundered through the corridor, causing us to jump apart. Even though the moment had been interrupted, I could feel the lingering heat of his body, the promise of what could have been.

A second later, a tabby sprinted past us in a blur of fur, executing a gravity-defying leap onto a nearby chair before catapulting out of an open window.

I blinked dazedly, trying to reorient myself.

What in the name of Mr. Darcy's tight breeches just happened?

"You okay, bookworm?"

I let out a nervous giggle. "Um, yeah." Never mind that he'd almost kissed me.

"Then come with me to the only room that has electricity."

Dax and I reentered the dining area, a space transformed under Dax's handiwork. A white sheet hung against the far wall, serving as an impromptu movie screen. The glow from the projector illuminated the room. He'd even unearthed a sofa from somewhere, brushing off years of neglect.

"Prepare yourself for cinematic greatness," Dax announced, waving an arm towards our setup for the evening.

"Is this the five-star experience you promised?"

"Only the best for my literary sparring partner." He bowed theatrically, then gestured at a bowl of popcorn and water bottles sitting on a table in front of the sofa. "It's not a movie without buttery calories. Besides, it's my cheat day."

I took a seat, plucking a kernel from the bowl and popping it into my mouth. The crunchy, salty taste was yummy., but it didn't distract me from that almost kiss.

Holy Heathcliff, I'd been mere seconds away from locking lips with Dax Granger. The same Dax who could charm the pants off a romance novel hero with his crooked grin and teasing quips. Not that I'd been fantasizing about him sans pants. Okay, maybe a little. But could you blame a girl? He was like a walking, talking amalgamation of my fictional boyfriends.

I snuck a glance at Dax as he fiddled with the projector.

The flickering light played across his chiseled features, making him look like he'd stepped straight out of a classic Hollywood film. I quickly pushed those lusty thoughts aside.

*Get it together, Paris.* It was just a movie night with a friend. A very attractive, charming friend who almost kissed you, but still. No need to go all Scarlett O'Hara swooning over here.

I was an overthinker, a planner. I didn't do spontaneity or risk-taking when it came to my heart. And I certainly didn't do romance, at least not outside the pages of my beloved books.

He sat on the sofa beside me, close enough that I could feel the warmth radiating off his body. We nestled into the surprisingly plush sofa cushions, and Dax hit play on the film projector. The opening credits of *It's Alive!* flickered to life, with the haunting strains of its score.

"Classic horror at its finest," he murmured.

I turned to Dax. "The author would be proud."

"Or she might take offense to the liberties the moviemakers have taken."

"Perhaps, yet adaptations are a form of flattery, right? A homage to the power of the original tale."

"Sounds exactly like something a bookworm would say."

His smile was infectious, and I smiled back. We watched the movie and munched on the popcorn. When the scene where the hero's lover dies, I clutched onto Dax's arm, then let go at his smirk.

After a few minutes, Dax turned to me, his expression unreadable in the dim light. "Um, Paris, can I ask you something?"

I nibbled on the popcorn. "Anything."

"Do you have a boyfriend?"

"Currently I'm in a complicated relationship with my TBR pile." I smiled, a hint of color rising in my cheeks. "I date on occasion, but nothing serious. You?"

"No, but I'm glad you're interested."

I snorted softly. "I'm not, not really. Any serious relationships?"

Dax reclined into the worn fabric of the couch, his gaze fixed on the movie, but his mind clearly elsewhere. "Nah. My addiction to true crime podcasts, fascination with decrepit mansions, and my weird habit of talking to my houseplants, like I've got my own *Little Shop of Horrors* might be too much for some girls."

"Be serious. Why nothing long-term?"

He sighed. "Well, maybe because I'm afraid they'll see the real me and bolt. Most girls think I'm all muscle and no brain. And not a guy who reads a lot."

I was the world's biggest hypocrite. I kept judging him for his love of horror and healthy lifestyle, while simultaneously lamenting that people often dismissed me as just another quirky cat lady and bibliophile.

"From what I've seen, you're kind, funny, and surprisingly insightful." My heart softened. "And have you seen *you*? You're hot. And I mean that in a totally objective, aesthetic appreciation kind of way, of course."

"Appreciate the compliments." His voice was low, raspy.

"Any girl would be lucky to have you. And if they can't handle the real you, than they're not worth your time."

He flashed a grin. "Guess we're too much for some people, huh? And you're right. It's about finding someone who wants the whole package."

Grabbing another handful of popcorn, I smiled. "Are you going to help me finish this buttery goodness?"

Dax laughed, reaching over to pluck a piece from the bowl. "Happy to oblige, bookworm."

The movie played on, the story tragic and spine-chilling. I was acutely aware of Dax beside me, our arms brushing with each shift, each shared glance a spark igniting a quiet fire in my chest. The muscles expanding his fitted T-shirt were more action hero than the studious boy-next-door types I usually swooned over.

My traitorous heart was betraying me, thumping hard. Because somehow, Dax was the most attractive man I'd ever met and also the scariest for that blood-pumping organ.

Sure, I liked Dax and was attracted to him. And yes, deep within me, I yearned to tumble headlong into a love story worthy of a Jane Austen heroine, but my doubts persisted. Dax was the type to leap first and look later, while I was more than likely to overthink myself into a stupor. Besides, I already knew how this story would end, with shattered illusions and a broken heart.

When the movie ended, I stretched my arms. "Well, as much as I'd love to stick around and see if this ghost shows up with a tray of otherworldly éclairs, I should probably head home. Sushi gets cranky if I'm late for her nightly belly rub session."

"Ah, of course. Can't keep the lady waiting. I'll just gather my stuff."

The boundaries of our friendship had blurred tonight, and the notion of relationships—once so clearly defined in my world—began to rewrite itself in the soft candlelight of a haunted hotel.

# Chapter Seven

*Dax*

STRETCHING, I HOISTED THE NOVEL, *LOVE Ledgers* above my head like a kettlebell—only this hardback wasn't exactly my speed. More romance than thrills, it felt out of place in my calloused hands. I tossed it on the leather couch with a grunt, the book thudding softly.

"Come on, Dax, it's just a guy and a girl, and they fall in love—what's not to get?"

The contrast between the flowery romance novel and my surroundings couldn't have been starker. My place was industrial-chic with leather furnishings, hardwood floors, and exposed brick walls, rough and unvarnished that matched my vibe. My gaze wandered to my collection of horror novels crammed onto the bookshelf—and I chuckled. They were probably judging me, their spines stiff with disapproval.

"Bet you didn't see this coming, huh?" I said to the thriller, suspense section. "Dax Granger, reading a romance novel."

Since when did I become a man who reads these things? Since Paris Novak.

Had to admit that joining the book club was ingenious. Like how I tackled a new client—assess the situation, gauge interest, and then go in for the kill. My plan had worked. Maybe a little too well because now I was slogging through this lovesick drivel, all because of wanting to know Paris better. I wasn't intimidated, just feeling out of my element.

An image of her flashed in my mind—that shiny, purple hair that resembled every sunset I'd ever seen. And those eyes, so blue they could slice right through you. She was a walking contradiction, witty and sharp, all wrapped up in a package so sexy it should come with a warning label.

Was I seriously crushing on a stubborn girl who only read romance?

*Damn.* Yeah, I was. Paris had this understated beauty and a quick wit, and the more I got to know her, the more I liked her.

Why else would I dive into a story that reveled in everything I'd always rolled my eyes at? Or maybe it was the way Paris talked about these novels, with such genuine passion, that made me want to be a part of whatever world she was living in.

*Hmmm.* Perhaps I'd learn a thing or two about winning her over. Or end up with paper cuts and a bruised ego.

With a deep breath, I dove back into the pages, determined to see this dare through to the end.

Hours later, I sucked in a breath, my back aching after being hunched over the book. The harsh noon light had mellowed and I hadn't budged, except for the occasional shift to alleviate the numbness in my glutes. I had to admit, *Love Ledgers* wasn't the sappy, unreadable drivel I'd expected, even if the subject matter wasn't my usual bowl of Wheaties.

Man, if the guys at the gym could see me now. The thought alone was enough to make me snort. They'd never let me live it down.

A solid knock at the door prompted me to set the book on the sofa.

When I swung it open, I grinned. My best buddy, William Graham, stood in the doorway with his broad, muscular frame. At thirty-eight, the guy still looked like he could take on a grizzly bear and come out on top. His square jaw and military-style buzz cut gave him that hardcore no-nonsense vibe. And those damn basketball shorts— I swear, the man would wear them in a blizzard if he could.

Since we had started working together at the gym, we'd been friends for over a decade. I had even been the best man at his wedding to Rachel, who happened to be one of Paris's closest friends. Yet, despite our long history, sometimes he just didn't get me.

William strode inside the loft, his cross-trainers silent on the hardwood floor. I shut the door and followed him into the living room. He claimed an armchair while I retook my seat on the couch, accidentally knocking the book to the floor.

"What is that, another fitness book?" William asked.

"It's a novel. A romance, if you can believe it." I tried to play it cool, but there was an edge to my voice like I was daring him to give me a hard time about it.

He snorted. "Wouldn't have pegged you for the Hallmark channel crowd."

"Neither did I, but here we are." I grabbed the book and set it on my thigh, tapping the cover with a finger. "There's actually some depth to this stuff. It's not all sentimental nonsense." A half-smile touched my lips. "And I haven't burst into flames yet."

"Depth, right." William snickered.

I tossed the book onto the coffee table and stretched my arms above my head. "Why are you here other than to bust my chops about expanding my reading choices?"

"Can't a friend drop by without an ulterior motive?" William asked, though his eyes were too sharp, too shrewd.

I sighed. "Lemme guess, you talked to your wife and she told you that I joined their book club."

William nodded. "She sure did and I had to come over and see if it was true. And I catch you reading a damn romance."

"It's not what you think. There's this reading challenge that I'm doing with Paris."

"My wife's friend?" William frowned. "The purple-haired pixie who eats donuts and has that weird cat?"

My jaw clenched. Paris was off-limits for cheap shots, even from a friend.

"Hey, don't knock the hair. It suits her. Or the cat." My tone was hard, biting.

He shook his head. "All right, all right. But why do I get the feeling there's more to this than reading touchy-feely books?"

"The truth is, she's got something about her. Beyond the obvious gorgeousness." I cleared my throat. "Paris... she's got this fire in her eyes, a sharp mind that keeps you on your toes. And she's damn sexy, no denying that. There's something that makes me want to figure her out. So, I joined the book club as a way to get to know her better."

William snickered, the sound like gravel tumbling down a hill. "And since when did you, a health nut get involved with someone like her? She doesn't even workout!"

"Since now, apparently." I scowled at him. "I like her. Had a crush on her since forever."

"Attraction is one thing, Dax, but romance novels? Book clubs?" William shook his head, bemusement carved into the lines of his face. "This is too weird, buddy."

Shrugging, I chuckled. "Heck, I'm not even sure I believe it myself. Me, the guy whose idea of a long-term commitment is a two-day hike. But, you know, it's not so bad."

William shook his head. "You should stick to fitness models. Leave the bookworms alone."

Irritation flared in my chest. How could he dismiss her so easily? He didn't know how her nose wrinkled when she laughed, or the way one rogue curl tumbled across her forehead when she was deep in thought.

"Paris...she's amazing." I frowned. "And she's your wife's best friend. I thought you liked her. Now you sound like she's a succubus out to steal my soul."

William grunted. "Hey, didn't mean to upset you. Paris is an okay girl. Just not for you, buddy."

"Define *not* for me." I crossed my arms.

"You're all about impromptu mountain climbs, treadmills, and scary movies, and she's..." William gestured vaguely as if her essence was something floating in the air like pollen. "Well, she's Paris, a woman who owns a bookshop specializing in romance novels, and most people in town think she's weird."

"She's just being herself. I like that about her."

William's brow furrowed. "I'm only looking out for you. You dive headfirst into everything. What happens when the novelty wears off? When she realizes you hate those romances she loves?"

"Maybe I don't anymore," I said strongly but my skin warmed.

"*Ha!*" William burst out laughing, slapping his knee. "You've gone insane."

"Shut up," I grumbled, the heat in my cheeks turning into a full-blown inferno. "It's about understanding what makes her tick, okay?"

"Look, you've been so preoccupied lately that I'm worried, dude. What's gonna happen to our weekend hikes and debating whether Bigfoot exists? Are you gonna be spending all your time with Paris now instead? Pals before gals!"

"Relax. Bigfoot does exist, and we can still hike. And maybe I want something else to talk about besides cryptids and muscle gains."

Willaim's concerns only fed my insecurities that I was just a horror-reading dude with a crush on a woman who probably perceived me as nothing more than the resident musclehead.

"I'm still the same guy. Just going after what I want and I *want* Paris." I slumped on the sofa and grunted, then snatched the book off the table. "But who am I kidding? She's out of my league."

For a moment, the only clamor was the distant hum of traffic and the soft creak of leather as I shifted on the couch.

My hands gripped the book tighter, and I could feel the imprint of the title pressing into my skin. I had dated plenty of beautiful women, but most were hollow and shallow on the inside. And there was no real connection outside the gym or looks. I wanted someone who had more to offer than sex and tossing compliments my way while they painted their lips and bragged about Botox injections.

My best friend frowned. "I just don't get it. The last

woman you dated was a smoking hot Swedish fitness model…now, you and that nerdy book girl…" His tone was more resigned than judgmental.

"Yeah."

He stood up, rolling his shoulders, a crack echoing through the loft. "Before I go, you still thinking about buying The Muscle Hut gym?"

"Thinking, yeah. Hoping more like it. Not sure I can get a loan on my own."

"Talk to your dad and see if he'll help. Just make a solid business plan first." William made his way to the door, then paused at the threshold. "Good luck with the reading challenge…and Paris."

I got up too, my limbs stiff. "Thanks."

He went out the door and it swung shut, leaving behind a silence that seemed louder than any of our conversations.

My thoughts drifted, as they often did these days, on Paris—her laughter, her beauty, her passion for stories I'd only begun to understand. The genre swap was about laying down the first bricks on a path that could lead in the right direction—a shot at something genuine with Paris.

Yet, the fear of rejection, of discovering my feelings were nothing more than one-sided, felt worse than when I sprained my ankle playing baseball. Sure, there was a chance I might strike out, but even the best athletes miss a swing sometimes. That didn't mean I wouldn't step up to the plate.

# Chapter Eight

THE CARNIVAL MIDWAY WAS A DIZZYING explosion of color and commotion. Neon signs flickered like they were having a rave, while the delicious smells of deep-fried *everything* assaulted my senses.

The flashing lights shimmered across Dax's handsome features, making him look like some modern-day Adonis...if he had a thing for funnel cakes and rigged carnival games. Tonight I felt a strange sense of adventure. Or I just really, really wanted to see him win me a giant stuffed unicorn.

Dax gestured toward the Ferris wheel, its lights blinking steadily. "Reminds me of a scene from *Love Ledgers*."

"It does, doesn't it? Is that why we're here?"

"Yep. I figured if we were going to do this right, we had to recreate a scene from each book we read. And what better way to celebrate finishing my first romance novel than with a classic carnival date?"

I tried to suppress a grin. "Well, I suppose I can't argue with that logic."

"Admit it, Paris, you're a sucker for romantic gestures and carnivals."

"Maybe." The atmosphere made it tempting to lean into the fantasy. "*If* this were a date, but it isn't, so it's less complicated."

We passed a juggler tossing balls into the air.

"And would that be so bad?"

I dodged a sticky-handed child barreling toward the cotton candy stand. "I guess not...although wouldn't it be nice if real-life romance came with a script? One penned by a hopeless romantic author who always delivers that perfect fairy tale ending, no matter how hopeless things seem at first. Swoon-worthy declarations of love, dramatic reunions in the rain, the whole shebang."

Alas, in the unscripted world of modern dating, I knew finding a soulmate was less "love at first sight" and more "falling in love, then swiping right." We were left to navigate the twists and turns of relationships without a roadmap.

"Sure, a guaranteed happily ever after would be comforting. But where's the fun in predictability?" he shot back, with a slow smile. "You've gotta change up your routine to keep things interesting, shock your muscles or you'll plateau."

I raised an eyebrow at him. "Are we still talking about romance, or did you just slip into personal trainer mode? Because I'm pretty sure my heart doesn't need a cardio workout right now."

"Okay, I'll leave my metaphors at the gym." He looked me up and down, then smiled. "Nice shirt. I should be flattered you agreed to come out with me tonight."

Today's ensemble: a graphic tee that boasted '*Bookmarks are for Quitters*,' paired with skinny jeans and my scuffed low-top sneakers.

Placing one hand on my hip, I stuck it out. "Yes,

consider yourself lucky. It's not every day a girl puts her fictional boyfriends on hold for a little carnival fun. And I figured even the most riveting chapter can't compare to the thrill of seeing you lose at ring toss."

"Oh, it's on now, bookworm."

Dax and I wove through the crowd, his arm slipping around my waist. I leaned into him, hyperaware of his solid strength. Each place our bodies met felt electric, making my skin tingle. It was as if every nerve ending in my body had jolted awake.

The sugary aroma of spun cotton candy teased my senses and I inhaled deeply. "*Mmm*, just smell that childhood nostalgia."

Dax's thumb traced distracting circles over my hip bone. "You mean empty calories?"

"Hey, some of us appreciate the finer things in life." I nudged him playfully. "Like deep-fried deliciousness and winning oversized stuffed toys."

He smirked. "Ah, the magic of clogged arteries."

"Not surprising the personal trainer advocates for balanced meals..." I froze, sniffing the air. "What's that smell—*oh*, corn dogs!" I led the way, guiding us through throngs of people clustered around game booths and rides.

Dax shook his head, faux concern etching his brow. "Paris, you're drooling."

A giggle escaped me, betraying my feigned indignation. "Am not! That's just, uh, preemptive taste-testing." I plowed ahead. "Let's make a pact—no leaving until we've tried all the essentials."

"What do you mean?"

"Popcorn, cotton candy, and anything that comes on a stick."

Dax groaned and extended a pinkie toward me. "You're going to ruin my diet, but okay."

"*Yay!*" I curled my pinkie around his. "First the games."

"Just so you know, I happen to excel at carnival games."

"Care to prove it?"

"Oh, yeah." Dax's laugh rumbled deep in his chest.

Spotting a carnival game booth, I tugged on his hand with a mischievous grin. "Ooh, let's do this one! I bet I can beat you." I snatched a toy water gun and took aim at the moving ducks, my tongue poking out the side of my mouth in an exaggerated look of concentration. Water sprayed everywhere as I enthusiastically squeezed the trigger, hitting everything except the targets.

He chuckled. "Paris, you crack me up. I never thought I'd meet someone who could make me laugh as much as you do."

"And I never thought I'd find someone who appreciates my sense of humor." I paused in front of the booth festooned with stuffed animals begging to be won. "Ring toss?"

Dax rolled up his sleeves, the flex of his muscles not lost on me—or my suddenly parched throat. "Watch and learn, bookworm. I'm about to win you the biggest, fluffiest one they have."

Giggling, I secretly hoped he'd win the whole darn booth. "Your confidence is as outsized as your biceps."

With focused concentration, he narrowed his gaze, picked up the rings and flicked his wrist, sending each one spinning toward the bottles. When one finally encircled its glassy neck, I cheered. He winked at me, and my heart did an acrobatic leap.

"Never doubted you for a second."

"Which one?" He gestured at the plush creatures hanging behind the carny—a menagerie of faux fur and stitched smiles.

"Surprise me."

After a moment's consideration, Dax reached for a purple octopus. "Ah, this one can hold a book in each hand—practical and cute."

"I love it." I clutched the stuffed toy to my chest. "Come on, let's pop some balloons."

"Sure you can handle the competition?"

"You might be king of the ring toss, but my aim is legendary," I boasted, even as my palms grew clammy.

At the booth, he handed me a dart. "Guess we'll see about that."

The game was simple; the feelings were not.

We threw darts, popping balloons with satisfying bursts. I caught myself stealing glances at him—the way his smile crinkled his eyes, the sharp line of his jaw.

"Your turn." He passed me another dart, his hand lingering over mine.

My dart found its mark, the balloon giving way with a loud pop. "Yes!"

Dax clapped. "Damn, you keep surprising me."

"Admit it, you didn't think I'd be this good."

"I've learned my lesson. Never underestimate Paris Novak." He bowed theatrically, making me laugh.

"Now, about those essentials we talked about." I grabbed his hand, leading him away from the games.

"Starting with?"

"Cotton candy—pink, please." I pointed to the vendor swirling clouds of sugar onto paper cones.

"Then pink it shall be." Dax procured a fluffy bloom, handing it to me.

"Thanks." I took a bite, the sugary strands dissolving on my tongue. A speck of pink clung to my lip, and I wiped it away with the back of my hand.

"Missed a spot."

His thumb gently swiped the corner of my mouth and my breath hitched. I took a step back and blew out a breath, tempering the giddy rush swelling inside me.

This attraction for Dax was disconcerting—someone who couldn't be more different from me if he tried. A buff jock and a romance junkie like myself? What were the odds?

Sometimes our clash of diversity felt like the opening gambit in a game that neither of us knew the rules to yet. It was those small differences, sure, but I wondered how many small differences it took to build a wall too high to climb—even for someone with Dax's persistence.

But for tonight, I just wanted to have fun and enjoy the twinkling lights, the screams from ride-goers, and the energy surrounding us.

He turned to me with a curious expression. "I've been wondering why you're still single. You must have men lining up at the bookshop door, eager to ask you out."

Shaking my head, I let out a snort. "Oh yes, it's a regular romance novel convention. I can barely keep up with all the suitors vying for my attention between the shelves."

Dax chuckled, but his eyes remained fixed on mine. "Seriously, why hasn't some lucky guy snatched you up yet?"

My smile vanished, my gaze dropping to the ground. "Let's just say I've had my fair share of romantic entanglements. And not the good kind."

Dax's fingers lightly lifted my chin, then lowered to entwine our fingers. "Do you want to talk about it? I'm a good listener while also being a dashing carnival companion."

I frowned, but felt some of the tension ease from my shoulders at his touch. "It's just...I've been hurt in the past. And when I was a teenager, my parents separated for a year. It was a rough time, and I guess it left some scars, making me cautious when it comes to relationships."

Dax nodded, his thumb tracing soothing circles on the back of my hand. His gentle touch ignited a warmth that spread through my veins.

We kept walking and passed a colorful fortune teller tent. My attention momentarily caught on a glowing sign outside.

"Did your parents ever reconcile after that year apart? I can only imagine how tough that must have been for you, especially as a teenager."

I huffed out a breath and pulled my hand from his. "They did, eventually. They live in Florida now, and the experience left me with some trust issues. And then there was the author..."

"Who's that?"

Recalling the memory, a wave of humiliation crashed over me, causing my cheeks to burn. "A year ago this writer, Julian Hale, came to the bookshop for a signing. I had always been a big fan of his work and was thrilled when he agreed to visit our small town. We ended up talking for hours that night, and it turned out he was visiting family here for the summer while he worked on a new book. We had this instant connection, and before I knew it, we were dating. It got serious fast...then everything started to unravel."

Dax's brow furrowed. "What happened?"

Every time I thought of Julian, a cold, leaden weight

settled in the pit of my stomach, as if I'd swallowed a ball of lead that refused to budge.

My hands shook, so I stuffed them into my pockets. "Um, Julian would often cancel plans at the last minute or become distant. While browsing through social media one day, I stumbled upon a post on Julian's feed from his fiancée gushing about their upcoming wedding plans. I was devastated. He had lied to me and I was just a temporary distraction for him. Since then, I've been cautious about letting anyone get close to me."

Dax's jaw clenched. "What a jerk. You didn't deserve that."

I shrugged, trying to play it off even as the old hurt resurfaced. "It's fine. It's not like I was naming our kids or anything, but it made me rethink the whole 'happily ever after' thing. It's hard to believe in fairy tales when reality keeps smacking you in the face."

He halted, his calloused hands firmly cupping my face. "Listen up, Paris. You're one heck of a woman. Smart as a whip, funnier than anyone I know, and beautiful inside and out. And if some idiot can't see that, then that's his loss."

Tears stung my eyes, overwhelmed by the sincerity in his voice. "You really mean that?"

He smiled, a soft, tender expression. "Every word. You deserve nothing less."

My heart flopped around in my chest. I leaned into hands, his touch warming my skin that had nothing to do with the spring weather. "You know what, Dax? I'm glad we're friends."

For a second, his smile faltered before locking back into place, a momentary pinch to the corners of his eyes. He lowered his arms. "Yeah. Me too."

Making our way through the crowd, I glanced at Dax.

"The carnival was a fun idea, which reminds me. How did you enjoy *Love Ledgers*?"

"For a romance, it was..." Dax hesitated. "Well, it wasn't nearly as painful as I thought it would be. In fact, I might even go so far as to say I enjoyed it. But don't let that go to your head. I'm still a hardcore horror guy."

I shook my head at his reluctant admission. It was like a vampire admitting sunlight wasn't so bad after all.

"I'm impressed. Not many people can jump from horror to romance without breaking a sweat."

Dax chuckled, shaking his head. "Or vice versa. Reading that book made me appreciate the little moments more. Like this one, right here, with you."

My heart did a little jig in my chest, even as my ever-pragmatic brain tried to blame it on the thrill of the carnival. He was just caught up in the moment, and it didn't mean anything more than that. We had nothing in common. He was a free-spirited gymgoer, and I was a cautious overthinker who alphabetized her spice rack for fun. I'd been burned before, and I wasn't about to let myself get swept up in another ill-fated love affair.

We ambled past booths in the direction of the rides. I sidestepped a group of giggling teenagers. The carnival lights glittered like a constellation of stars as we joined the line for the Ferris wheel.

I glanced up at him. "Dax, tell me about your family."

"Um, my dad was a high school football coach when I was younger. When he retired, he invested in stocks and made a lot of money over the years." His voice was tinged with respect and distance. "Growing up, he was tough, disciplined. He loved sports and teaching young people to push their limits."

"And your mom?"

"She was the softer side of home." Dax grinned, his expression lighting up. "A librarian. Kind-hearted, always lost in books. Guess that's where I got my love of reading." His chuckle echoed in the cool night air.

Intrigued by the contrast of his parents' influences, I smiled. It painted a picture of a home filled with discipline and dreams, a breeding ground for someone as multifaceted as Dax was turning out to be.

"As the youngest of three, I always felt like I had something to prove," he continued, his gaze taking in the crowd. "My two hotshot older brothers were these high achievers in sports, grades, whatever. I guess it made me competitive, always chasing the appeal of perfection."

I studied his profile, glimpsing the remnants of that younger Dax, striving to step out from the shadows of his siblings.

"Did it ever feel like too much? Trying to keep up?"

He blew out a breath, a nakedness flashing through his stare. "All the time. It's like wearing a mask, you know? Showing confidence when inside you're wondering if you'll ever measure up." He cleared his throat. "My dream is to own the local gym and offer free fitness programs to underprivileged kids. Fitness has become my way of helping others find their strength, not just physically but within themselves."

His honesty struck a chord in me. The Ferris wheel line moved, but we were anchored in a moment of raw truth. Dax's journey, his battles against insecurities, and the drive to forge his own path, which I totally respected. It was a story of resilience, seeking to redefine himself beyond family expectations.

"It takes a lot of courage to follow a dream. Those kids will be fortunate to have someone like you in their corner."

He shrugged. "Yeah. That's the dream someday."

Standing there amidst the whirling rides and the stench of stale popcorn, it seemed that Dax was more than just a pretty face. When he'd spoken of family rivalry and personal ambitions, I felt an intense affection for him. It was like we were both searching for our own identity and place in the world. Maybe we were both a little lost, a little vulnerable, and a lot determined to figure out this whole adulting thing.

Finally reaching the front of the line, we handed our tickets to the attendant and boarded the waiting gondola. The wheel lurched into motion, and we were lifted off the ground, the world below us shrinking with every breath. The fairground sprawled beneath us—winking lights, miniature people, the echo of music weaving through the night—and for a fleeting second, everything felt possible. Then again, it could just be the altitude going to my head.

"Beautiful, isn't it?"

"Nothing compared to—" He stopped mid-sentence and shook his head with a snicker. "Man, that was going to sound incredibly cheesy."

I nudged his arm "Now I gotta know what you were gonna say."

"Nothing compared to the view right here." He gestured at me. "Because being with you, sharing this moment, it feels like everything I've ever wanted and never knew I needed."

A hot flush rose in my cheeks. I opened my mouth to respond, then clamped it shut. Even though my heart fluttered at his sentiment, a tiny voice whispered a warning. Was I ready to trust someone again, to open myself up to the possibility of heartbreak?

Okay, sure, Dax was charming and sweet, but the last

thing I needed was another chapter in the saga of Paris's disastrous love life. I mean, really, who gave him the right to waltz into my life with his brawny physique and charming smile, throwing off my perfectly balanced equilibrium?

"Very smooth. If I didn't know better, I'd think you were trying to charm your way into another outing."

"Maybe I am," he whispered.

Peering over the side, I pretended like I hadn't heard him.

The Ferris wheel carried us aloft, and the summit drew nearer until we crested the apex. At the top, the gondola swayed gently, suspended in a pocket of time where the world below seemed about as significant as a gnat on a windshield.

"Hey, bookworm?" Dax said softly.

The ride spun downward, the ground getting closer and closer.

"Yeah?"

"Thank you for tonight. I can't remember the last time I had this much fun."

"Me too. I'm glad we did this."

"Now, what do you say we go find some deep-fried Oreos to munch on?"

"What about your strict diet?"

Dax threw his hands up. "Tonight's a free carb and sugar pass. I'll hit the gym early tomorrow and work it off."

He was only doing this for me and I knew how passionate he was about his health and fitness. I almost felt guilty for corrupting him. Almost.

I smirked. "Prepare to be dazzled by my iron stomach and unparalleled junk food consumption."

Stepping off the Ferris wheel, I sensed a shift between us —like the universe had decided to play cosmic matchmaker.

Except I wasn't exactly the type to swoon over a hardbody —okay, maybe just a little swooning, and could anyone blame me?

But I had to tamp down on those feelings and keep him in the friend zone. Things were complicated enough.

# Chapter Nine

THE MORNING SUN SLANTED THROUGH THE GAUZY curtains of my cottage home, coloring the vintage furnishings that I'd curated from flea markets and estate sales in a soft yellow light.

I sank into the plush cushions of the sofa reading *Emma* while I ate my cinnamon roll and drank a cup of vanilla coffee. Sushi scrutinized me from her plush cat bed near the fireplace. I was just settling into the story when Sushi let out a plaintive meow. She hopped up onto the couch and plopped herself right on top of the open pages of my book.

"Excuse me, Your Highness." I quirked an eyebrow at her. "Is there something I can help you with?"

Sushi blinked at me lazily, then pointedly turned her head to look at the photo laying on the end table—a silly strip of photo booth pictures of Dax and me from the carnival last night. Our cheeks were flushed from laughter and perhaps one too many sugar-spun funnel cakes.

My face warmed at the memory. "It was just two friends hanging out, nothing more."

Sushi's golden eyes narrowed as if to say, '*Oh, please.*'

"Fine. Maybe it was more fun than I anticipated. It doesn't mean anything."

Doesn't it though?

"Stop it, brain. We're *not* doing this!" I petted Sushi's soft fur, causing snowy-white tufts to float around me. "Dax is all biceps and bravado, and I'm...well, not. I can't even do a pull-up and I love junk food!"

Was I being too hasty in writing off the potential of a real-life love story?

"Okay, so I'm attracted to him—now what? We're too different...aren't we?" I sighed. "Well, except that he makes me laugh, and his passion for reading, albeit creepy subjects, matches mine."

"Meow." Sushi blinked up at me, which I took as a reminder that opposites did attract.

"Who knew a night of cotton candy and ring tosses could leave me so upside down?" I slipped my copy of *Emma* from beneath Sushi. "I need a dose of predictability where the biggest worry is miscommunication, not the confusing reality of...whatever this is with Dax Granger."

I couldn't let myself get carried away by a handsome face and a disarming smile.

"Meow." Perhaps my cat understood the complexities of human relationships better than I did.

I tried to focus on *Emma*, but kept lowering the book. Another rested on the table, a novel Dax had recommended as my second horror read. I just couldn't bring myself to start it yet.

Glancing at the clock, I frowned. I'd be late for work unless I got going. Stretching, I grabbed my purse and Sushi, and then left the house.

Strolling along Main Street with Sushi resting on my

shoulder, I took in the quaint storefronts and charming cafes. The air, an aroma of bluebells—the town's namesake —wafted on the spring breeze. In a town this size, everyone not only knew each other, but also your coffee order and the name of your Wi-Fi network.

At the bookstore, I unlocked the door and stepped inside, letting my cat loose to roam while I went behind the counter and tidied the display of bestsellers.

The bell above the door chimed, announcing the arrival of Peregrine Downey, a regular patron whose eclectic tastes never failed to bring a smile to my face. Her electric shock of white hair stood on end, her eyes bright behind thick-rimmed glasses.

"Why, hello there, Paris!" Peregrine's long fingers gesticulated wildly. "I must say, I always adore the ambiance of this establishment. It simply *tickles* my literary sensibilities. Now, have you chanced upon any *deliciously* obscure tomes that might pique my *ravenous* appetite for the written word?"

I grinned at her enthusiasm. "Peregrine, I believe I have just the book for you." I moved from behind the counter, my fingers skimming the spines until I found the perfect match. "Have you read '*Corsets, Carriages, and Courtship*' by Diane Chesterfield? It's a historical romance I think you'll enjoy."

Peregrine's eyes widened. She accepted the book, read the back jacket, and then smiled. "Why, this sounds *positively* delectable! You are a true literary *matchmaker*. Like Emma Woodhouse, but with books instead of beaus."

I laughed, the comparison to Jane Austen's heroine was both flattering and amusing. As an avid fan of *Emma*, I had a kinship with the meddlesome matchmaker. Of course, my interfering involved less romantic entanglements and more literary liaisons. If it brought joy and a love of reading to the people of Bluebell Bend, than I was happy to help.

"I pride myself on finding the perfect book for every reader. It's my own brand of matchmaking magic."

"Oh, I most *ardently* agree! Thank you for the thoughtful recommendation."

I glanced at my cat perched atop a nearby shelf.

"What do you think, Sushi? Should I embrace my inner Emma and start arranging blind dates between lonely books and forlorn readers?"

Sushi meowed, her tail swishing in what I chose to interpret as approval.

She looked from me to the cat. "Paris? Are you *conversing* with me or the cat?"

"Um. Both?" I went to the register. "Your total is thirteen dollars and two cents."

Peregrine drew back, her eyes widening in horror as if I'd just told her that her hair was on fire. "*No*. No, that will not do. Thirteen? Are you sure? I won't have that number *defiling* my purchase. You're trying to *curse* me. Well, I won't stand for it! Either change that total *or* I'll find a bookstore that doesn't want me to get hit by a falling piano or attacked by a swarm of angry bees!"

I blinked, trying to keep a straight face. "Um, I apologize for any inconvenience. Let me see what I can do." I fiddled with the register, pretending to make adjustments. "There we go! Twelve, ninety-nine. Crisis averted, and your luck remains intact."

She sniffed, eyeing me suspiciously as she handed over the money. "Good. I'll be *watching* you, young lady. I don't like to believe town gossip, but they say you and your shop are *irregular*. So, one *whiff* of bad mojo and I'll be back, sage and crystals in hand!"

Peregrine paid for her purchase and marched out the door. I looked at Sushi and shrugged.

Determined to focus on work, I started organizing the cowboy romance section, yet my brain had other plans. It insisted on replaying every moment of my non-date with Dax at the carnival in vivid, heart-fluttering detail. His tender smile, the way his hand felt in mine...and I couldn't stop a silly grin

*No, no, no!* I mentally scolded myself, shaking my head as if trying to physically dislodge the thoughts.

Sushi leaped onto the counter and fixed me with an unblinking stare.

"Don't give me that look." I scratched behind her ears. "I'm not falling for anyone, especially not a personal trainer who probably thinks Austen is a brand of workout gear."

"Meow."

"Yes, thank you for the support."

*Huh.* Did people in town find me strange because I spoke to my cat as if she understood me?—which she totally did. Perhaps that was just another quirk to add to the long list of things that made me stand out in Bluebell Bend.

And yet, as much as I embraced my uniqueness, there was still a part of me longing for a connection—someone who would appreciate my quirks and love me not despite them, but because of them.

The door opened. Cassius Flinn, a man in his early fifties, trudged into the store. He wore a tweed jacket, a slightly askew bowtie, and bright yellow socks peeking out from the hem of his slacks. Cassius owned the dry cleaner's next door and he was always petitioning the town council to get me to paint my shop a more neutral color. So far, I'd successfully defended my right to keep my shop's cheery pink exterior.

"Welcome to Prose & Positivity!" I called out, with my best bookshop owner smile.

"Ah, Paris!" he exclaimed, eyeing my outfit. "Still sporting that quirky style of yours, I see."

I tugged down my graphic T-shirt that read, '*Books Are My Love Language*,' and shrugged. "Guess I'm a trendsetter."

Sushi yawned, scrutinizing Cassius with a touch of both aloofness and disdain.

The man frowned. "I don't think I'll ever understand you. You're not exactly what people expect from a respectable businesswoman in Bluebell Bend."

My fists clenched. The all-too-familiar sting of being dubbed as an outsider left a bitter taste in my mouth. It wasn't the first time someone had pointed out how I didn't quite fit in with the rest of the town.

I plastered on a smile. "Oh, I'm not here to blend in with the wallpaper. I'm the splash of color that keeps Bluebell Bend from being a complete snoozefest. Besides, if I started conforming to expectations now, I'm pretty sure the town gossips would die of shock, and we can't have that on our consciences, can we?"

"Ah, but there's a difference between being unique and being, well, odd. The purple hair, the funky pink color of your bookshop, and always talking to your cat...it's all so unconventional. You're a businessowner, young lady!" Cassius's tone took on a condescending edge. "You should act like one."

Sometimes it was tiring to constantly defend my choices and lifestyle. But then I thought of the joy my bookshop brought me, the comfort I found in my cat's companionship, and the exhilarating freedom of expressing myself authentically. Those things were worth a little small-town side-eye.

My shoulders straightened. "I'm not any different than any of you. I'm just not afraid to be myself."

Cassius smirked, his upper lip curling in a way that made me want to reach for the nearest book and chuck it at his smug face. "You might get more business if you tried blending in a tad more."

My body tensed and self-doubt crashed over me—fear that I was destined to be an outsider forever, never quite belonging. My thoughts shifted to Dax. He was different too, in his own way. A health nut obsessed with horror movies and books, trying to carve out his place in this small town. Perhaps we had more in common than I initially believed. We were both square pegs trying to fit into the round holes of Bluebell Bend's expectations.

I drew strength from the realization that I wasn't alone in my otherness. After all, hadn't Dax listened intently while I babbled on about the symbolic significance of floral imagery in Victorian literature on the drive home from the carnival?

Swallowing hard, I pushed back the lump forming in my throat. "I'd rather be true to myself than pretend to be someone I'm not, even if it means being misunderstood."

Cassius sighed. "Well, I suppose we all have our quirks. Some people collect stamps, others spend their days knitting sweaters for ceramic dolls. Not that I would know anything about that."

As tempting as it was to tell Cassius to take his unsolicited opinions elsewhere and show him the door, I took the high road. And a negative *Yelp* review might put a serious damper on my dreams of bookish world domination.

Mustering a smile, I said, "Now, what brings you in today?"

"I need a book for my niece's birthday. She's turning sixteen and I haven't the foggiest idea what girls her age like to read these days."

I tapped my chin, my thoughts already sifting through the countless titles lining the shelves. "I think I have just the thing." I led him to the classics section and plucked a copy of *Sense and Sensibility* from the shelf. "A classic tale of love and family drama. It's like a 19th-century version of 'The Bachelorette,' but with more corsets and fewer hot tubs. Trust me, your niece will love it."

Handing him the book, my spine straightened, proud of my ability to find the perfect book for every reader. I was the ultimate book matchmaker, and maybe being different wasn't such a bad thing after all.

# Chapter Ten

T HE  WASHER'S  BUZZER  JOLTED  ME  FROM  MY
reading reverie. Seated in the local laundromat, I had been
thoroughly engrossed in *Rosemary's Babysitter* by Ivan
Leery. Placing my bookmark inside the page, I stood up and
glanced at the clock made from a repurposed detergent box.

Scuffed linoleum tiles covered the floor, and retro
artwork decorated the walls. Bright fluorescent lighting illuminated the multicolored clothing and linens whirling
behind the round windows of the washers.

The door swung open, and Dax entered with a lopsided
grin, holding a mesh bag of dirty clothes. "Ah, my favorite
bookworm, venturing out from her literary lair to tackle the
laundry beast."

"Hey, Dax." My heart skipped a disturbed beat.

"And I thought I was the only one who liked to mix
fabric softener with my horror novels." He jerked his chin
at the paperback lying on top of my basket. "How are you
liking *Rosemary's Babysitter*? Has it started to creep you out
yet?"

Taking change from my pocket, I dumped quarters into

the dryer. "Only slightly more than the local gym instructor has."

He rolled his eyes, then hoisted his bag onto a counter. "Looks like we both had the same idea. Though I have to say, your choice of reading material is far more intriguing than my old sports magazines."

I held up the book, the cover featuring an eerie babysitter. "Horror novels and laundromats. The perfect combination for an exciting Friday night. Keeps me on the edge of my seat, wondering what's lurking in the shadows...or the lint trap."

Dax grinned. "So, am I right? Has the babysitter cast a spell on you yet?"

"No, but it's always nice to have someone checking to make sure I haven't joined an evil coven of childcare providers."

"I got you." His reply was immediate, sincere. "Pampers and holy water on standby. So, the book? What do you think so far?"

"The storyline's gripping and intense, and has an odd sense of romanticism."

"See?" Dax said, sorting his socks into piles. "Horror's not just about the scares and gore. Some have a touch of romance, too."

My eyebrow lifted. "Dax, if homicidal babysitters signify romance for you, we clearly need to work on your dating profile."

Dax leaned against a dryer. "Perhaps, it's time to redefine my idea of a meet-cute to include spellbooks and moonlit rituals."

I shook my head, transferring my clothes from the washer to the dryer. Leave it to Dax to find the romantic potential in occult activities. His ability to spin even the most outlandish scenarios into date ideas was both endearing and mildly concerning.

"Should I be worried about you showing up at my door with a bouquet of wolfsbane and a pentagram-shaped box of chocolates?"

He laughed. "Nah, I'm more slick than that."

"Oh, really? What's your approach then?"

Dax smirked. "Think less ritual sacrifice, more Netflix and hex. Maybe some popcorn for the full effect."

I snickered. "Of course, you'd find a way to make dark magic sound like a casual Saturday night."

Dax shrugged. "Why not? Life's too short to take everything so seriously."

I studied him, then grinned. His easygoing outlook was infectious, a welcome contrast to my tendency to overthink every little detail. Dax's presence was becoming a soothing balm, reminding me to find the humor and lightness in even the strangest of circumstances.

"I never thought I'd say this, but your laid-back attitude is starting to grow on me. It's like you have this superpower of finding the humor in even the most bizarre situations."

Dax grinned. "Someone has to balance out your high-strung tendencies, Miss Overthinking-Is-My-Middle-Name."

I shoved him, but he barely budged. Damn those rock-solid muscles. "Excuse me. I prefer to think of it as being charmingly neurotic. Seriously though, it's like you're my personal Zen master, minus the bald head and flowing robes."

He wiggled his eyebrows. "Do go on. What else do you like about me, bookworm?"

I rolled my eyes, trying to suppress a smile. Truth be told, his physique had definitely caught my attention initially. But as I got to know him, I discovered that Dax was so much more than a pretty face and chiseled abs. He had a heart of gold and a mind that never ceased to surprise me.

"Um, your compassion, humor, and generosity. And who would've thought that beneath those bulging biceps lies a philosopher?"

Dax clutched his chest. "Are you saying that you were only interested in my body at first? That hurts."

"Hardly. Well...maybe just a little." I laughed. You know, I gotta admit, I love our back-and-forth. It's pretty awesome having someone who can match my snarky comments and actually gets me to look at things differently."

"Wow, with praise like that, I might just have to propose right here among the fabric softener and dryer sheets," he joked.

The laundromat was quiet except for the hum of spinning machines. A woman entered with a bundle of laundry, mostly baby clothes, and started doing her wash at the other end of the room.

"Okay, so let's talk about *Rosemary's Babysitter*," I said. "We've got a witch eyeing Rosemary's tot like it's the last slice of pizza at a party. She's convinced snagging the kid will turbocharge her supernatural powers."

"Ah, but peel back the layers, and you'll find it's like a warped love letter, too." Dax dumped a capful of detergent into the washer and closed the lid. "The babysitter chose Rosemary out of all the women in the whole world to babysit for. It's like swiping right on destiny—if destiny had a fondness for the dark arts and murder."

Giggling, I tossed a dryer sheet into the machine. "I suppose there's a perverse charm in her relentless pursuit.

Like a postman, neither rain nor sleet nor dark of night could keep her from her coven duties."

"And yet, beneath her witchy exterior, her heart beats with desires unfulfilled, dreams of motherhood painted with a darker palette. Today's curse is tomorrow's enchantment." Dax nudged my arm with his.

I started the dryer. "If she ever decides to trade her broomstick for a minivan, I'm sure the PTA meetings would be a scream."

Dax chuckled. "Can you imagine? 'All right, ladies, today's agenda: bake sale, carpool schedule, and the annual sacrifice to the dark lord.'"

"And I bet she'd be the type to insist on organic, locally sourced eye of newt for the school potions lab."

We laughed. I retook my seat. Shafts of sunlight sliced through the windows, forming shifting patterns on the checkerboard linoleum floor.

He sat across from me on a hard plastic chair. "I have to say, Paris, our conversations on books and life are the highlight of my day."

"Well, I do have a PhD in witty banter and a black belt in sarcasm. But seriously, who else would indulge my passionate rants about proper bookshelf organization?" I shrugged, glancing down at the floor before meeting his eyes again. "And...you have a way of making me feel like the most fascinating person in the room, which is so sweet and appreciated."

"That's because you are fascinating, Paris." Dax leaned back, his voice soft, intimate. "Your passion, your kindness —it's remarkable. You have this way of making everyone who steps into your bookshop feel at home, like they're part of something bigger. That's a rare gift, and one I admire."

My cheeks burned so red I probably looked like I had a

major sunburn. I couldn't remember the last time someone had seen me so clearly, appreciating the very qualities that often made me feel like an outcast in Bluebell Bend. I could sense my resolve crumbling. Which meant I had to keep my guard up, even if it meant fighting what I felt for the man who seemed to understand me in a way no one else ever had

"With lines like that, it's a wonder you're not a romance novelist yourself."

He smiled. "Nah, I'm more of a 'speak from the heart' type of guy. And I just feel incredibly lucky to be your friend. To be a part of your life."

"Is that so? I figured you were more of a slow-burn, friends-to-lovers trope-y guy," I teased.

"Oh, I am." He shifted and the plastic chair squeaked. "I should probably let you get back to your laundry and babysitter from Hell."

Not what I wanted. At all. I couldn't let him slip away, not when I was enjoying his company so much.

"We can do ours together," I blurted, then, more quietly, "If you want." The words flew out of my mouth before I could second-guess myself.

Dax paused with a soft smile. "I'd like that."

"Good. I wasn't quite ready to face the laundry demons alone."

"Then I'll protect you from them. Fear not, fair maiden, for I shall hold back these cotton foes with my mighty dryer sheet shield."

Laying a hand on my forehead, I pretended to swoon. "My hero. Whatever would I do without you and your lint roller of justice?"

He stood and tossed his whites into an empty machine. "Well, for starters, you'd have to face the perils of static cling all by yourself."

It was the bantering moments like these with Dax that made my cheeks ache from smiling.

I gasped. "*The horror!* I might end up accidentally accessorizing with a dryer sheet."

"Don't worry, I've got your back, bookworm."

"My reputation as a fashionista is safe in your capable hands." I curtsied, nearly tripping over a cart in the process.

Dax laughed, steadying me with a hand on my arm. "Careful there. Don't want you taking a tumble on my watch."

His proximity was doing strange things to my heart, somersaults and backflips, that would score well in the Olympics of emotional turmoil. But I squashed those dangerous feels. Laundry awaited, and I couldn't risk turning into a walking lint trap.

"At least I know you'd be there to catch me. My very own knight to the rescue."

"I draw the line at jousting with ironing boards. A man's gotta have his limits."

I picked up a stray sock from the floor. "I suppose I can settle for a chivalrous dude who's handy with a bottle of stain remover."

"At your service, milady," Dax said with a playful bow.

He had a way of making even the most mundane tasks seem fun. With him around, I half expected a quirky musical montage to break out at any moment, complete with dancing laundry baskets and singing dryer sheets. And each time we hung out, a deeper connection formed between us. I liked that Dax genuinely understood and appreciated me for who I was—weird quirks, quips, and all.

"So, um...you ever think about the future?"

He leaned against the folding table. "All the damn time.

It's what keeps me motivated at the gym and in my personal life."

"Well, I have this dream of expanding my Instagram persona..." I paused, my nerves prickling at sharing my deepest ambition. "I, uh, I want to create a community that celebrates reading in all forms, a virtual place for booklovers to connect, explore, and find their next read."

"You should do it. You'd be great at that." His expression was sincere, encouraging.

"And I envision my bookshop becoming a landmark in Bluebell Bend," I said, warming to the theme. "A place where stories are not just sold but lived and experienced."

"That's awesome. I have no doubt you'll make it happen. Your bookshop is more than just a store, it's a place where people can be themselves. And that's because of *you*."

My heart swelled so quickly that I half expected to float off the ground and right up through the ceiling.

Could I actually be catching feels for this guy?

A surge of emotion threatened to overwhelm me. For so long, I had felt like someone who didn't quite fit in, but with Dax, I felt seen.

Without warning, a sudden, blistering pain shot through my temples, the start of a massive tension headache. An onslaught of unwanted memories insidiously filled my head. A reminder of what a fool I'd been. I'd trusted Julian completely, put all my faith in him, and he didn't deserve any of it. That whole mess with him left me with this festering wound, warning me not to get too carried away or trust guys too easily. The experience had left me torn between self-preservation and the urge to close myself off entirely. It was exhausting, and made me question *everything* with Dax.

Pushing aside those painful thoughts, I ducked my

head. "I have to admit, it's nice to know someone sees the magic in what I'm trying to create."

"I'm here for you, bookworm." He grinned, holding up a pair of mismatched socks. "Even if it means pondering the great sock mystery. Seriously, where do all the missing ones go?"

I shrugged. "I've heard rumors of a secret society, where all the lost socks gather to plot their escape from the tyranny of the dryer."

"Ah, so that's where they all end up! I knew there had to be a logical explanation."

"If it's true, I've got a few pairs that could use some reuniting. For now, I'll just have to embrace the mismatched look." I held up two wildly different socks, one striped and one polka-dotted.

"I'm sure you'll start a new trend in Bluebell Bend."

We were quiet for a moment, sorting our laundry. The room was filled with the steady hum of the washers and dryers, punctuated by the occasional clang of buttons and zippers. Fluorescent lights buzzed overhead. I caught a whiff of fabric softener blended with the scent of lavender detergent.

"So, I've been thinking, if *Rosemary's Babysitter* had an Instagram, what do you think she'd post? Moody brew potion selfies?"

I snorted. "Hashtag witch-tastic lifestyle."

"Hashtag murderous for likes."

We laughed. Dax's chuckle was a husky baritone that melted my insides.

"In all seriousness," he said, "I've noticed how much effort you put into your bookstagram. It's impressive."

"Much appreciated." I toyed with the cat charm bracelet on my wrist that Aunt Margo had given me, the cool metal soothing against my fingertips. "It started as just a hobby, you know? Now it's...more."

"What do you mean?" He leaned in, so close I could count the golden flecks in his eyes. His spicy cologne teased my senses, woodsy with a hint of citrus.

"More as in my account could be *something*. Real and big, but...it's all kinda...I don't know..." My voice faltered. I knew what I wanted to say, and of what I was afraid to admit.

"Overwhelming?" His thumb brushed against the back of my hand, rough calluses against my softer skin.

"Yeah, that." I half-laughed, half-choked on the truth of it.

His hand still enveloped mine, strong, steady, and sure. I never wanted him to let go. Silence lingered between us, ripe and heavy with emotion.

"Paris?" Dax's tone was a gruff rumble, sending tingles to all the right places.

"Mmm?"

"Once you finish *Rosemary's Babysitter*, would you like to visit Eternal Slumber Cemetery with me? The book's climax unfolds in a graveyard, so I thought it would be a fitting excursion for our next outing."

"A graveyard date?" I smiled. "Sure, Dax. I'd love to get spooky with you."

He gave my hand a final squeeze, his touch searing into my skin like a brand, before releasing me. The loss of contact was acute, like a physical ache. I flexed my fingers, already missing the weight of his hand in mine.

Dax was the romantic plot twist that I never saw coming, and I was starting to suspect that resistance might be futile.

# Chapter Eleven

OVER THE NEXT FEW WEEKS, DAX AND I SPENT more and more time together. Between our genre debates and laundry rendezvouses, I was peeling back the layers of the muscle-bound man who had become my favorite partner in crime. And I appreciated having a chauffeur for our outings.

It was nice to have a friend with a reliable car and an encyclopedic knowledge of the best bakeries in town. Well, there were only two bakeries in Bluebell Bend, but we frequently visited them both and still couldn't decide which one was better.

Beyond Dax's impressive ability to parallel park in the tightest of spaces, I admired his work ethic and love of reading. And when he impressed me with his soft spot for felines? Let's just say, I started liking him even more.

Who would've thought that I'd find such a kindred spirit in a man who could probably bench press a small car?

While I waited for Dax to pick me up, I angled the paperback closer to the black plastic cauldron I'd dug out from my Halloween décor. The title *Rosemary's Babysitter* emblazoned across the book cover caught the last rays of sunlight. A perfect shot for my bookstagram account. Peering through my phone camera, my lips puckered in a mock-serious pout.

*Just brewing up some literary magic. Don't worry, no actual babysitters were harmed in the making of this post*, I captioned the photo and hit share.

Instantly, 'likes' began to trickle in.

"Attempting to lure in new followers?"

Dax stepped through the door and flashed me a crooked grin that made my knees feel like they'd been replaced by Jell-O.

I set my phone down on the coffee table. "You know me, just sharing my love for literature with the world."

Dax plopped down on the couch. "Just as long as you haven't accidentally summoned any fictional characters to life after reading that book. You have no idea how persuasive those Ouija boards can be."

Gasping in mock offense, I swatted his arm. "Excuse *you*, I am a responsible reader. I would only summon the most well-behaved characters. Unlike *you*."

He placed a hand over his heart, feigning a wounded expression. "*Ouch*. And here I thought you kept me around for my devastating good looks and rapier-sharp wit."

I snorted, grabbing a throw pillow and hugging it to my chest. "More like your uncanny ability to find the best parking spots."

Dax draped an arm across the back of the couch. "Call me a man of many talents. And if those talents happen to include protecting you from meter maids, then so be it."

"What would I do without you?"

"Probably be drowning in parking tickets. Face it, Paris. You need me."

Tossing the pillow at him, he caught it with ease. "Need is a strong word. I prefer *tolerate*. And only because you have a car and I don't."

He snorted. "I thought we had something special. I'm wounded, truly."

"Oh, stop being so dramatic. You know you've become one of my favorite people, even if you do have questionable taste in pizza toppings."

He threw the pillow back at me, which I narrowly dodged. "Says the woman who thinks cat fur is a fashion statement."

Glancing down at my shirt, I frowned. "I'll have you know that I'm single-handedly keeping the lint roller industry in business. It's a sign of my unwavering devotion to my feline overlord."

He stood and moved closer, his gaze soft and warm. Raising his hand, he gently brushed hair behind my ear. I drew back, my breath catching in my throat.

"Ready to go, bookworm?"

Nodding, I grabbed my bag, tucking my phone and the copy of *Rosemary's Babysitter* inside before heading out.

Dax and I hopped into his car and drove across town. Streetlamps flicked on, the last vestiges of sunset clinging to the rooftops in fiery patches. He parked the car down the street and we continued on foot. The evening was cool enough for my breath to form puffs in the air, yet tepid enough that the chill felt refreshing rather than biting.

A graveyard loomed ahead, its wrought-iron gates doused in moonglow. An owl hooted from a tree and a ground fog churned around our legs.

Dax rested his hand on the gate. "May I introduce you to Eternal Slumber Cemetery."

The gates screeched open, and Dax and I stepped inside.

Hanging out with Dax tonight was kind of exciting. Though I wasn't ready to admit it aloud, horror was beginning to grow on me—like a fungus, but in a good way.

We ventured deeper into the cemetery, where the lampposts emitted an otherworldly luminosity, turning the tombstones silver. The breeze carried the scent of earth and old stone.

Dax glanced up at the full moon. "I could see you having an epic romance with a brooding vampire."

"And you'd be the wisecracking werewolf who keeps sabotaging our relationship."

Dax placed a dramatic hand over his heart. "I'd prefer to think I'd be the adorable sidekick who helps you realize that he's the wolf for you. Team werewolf for life!"

Smacking my forehead with one hand, I scoffed. "Oh, *please*. You'd be constantly distracted by squirrels and fire hydrants. I think I can navigate the supernatural dating scene on my own."

A contented sigh escaped me, delighted to be wandering through the cemetery—of all places—with this wonderful, exceptional man by my side. It felt surprisingly intimate sharing this space with him, surrounded by memories carved in stone.

"I wonder what their stories were," I whispered, reading the faded inscriptions. Some names were still legible, others were lost to time. "Dax, did you ever imagine yourself as the good guy in horror novels as a kid?"

He was quiet a moment, then cleared his throat. "Yep. Always the hero, never the victim. And you?"

"I'm the stealthy woman with a hidden agenda. The one who everyone underestimates until she saves the day with her obscure knowledge of ancient rituals and her clever cat."

"Ah, a woman of layers and intrigue."

"Like an onion." I tilted my head. "Or a parfait. Everybody loves parfaits."

Dax and I wandered past crumbling headstones, flower wreaths, and angel effigies. The lampposts' soft light created an eerie ambiance. Like a scene straight out of a Tim Burton film, where a skeleton might pop out, ready to serenade us with a jazzy tune about the joys of being dead.

"So, did you bring garlic and crosses?"

"Of course." Dax patted his back pocket. "It's what makes me a great personal trainer. Being prepared is the key to success, whether it's for a workout or a graveyard stroll."

"Where are we going?"

Dax pointed to a mausoleum at the far end of the cemetery, its marble façade gleaming under the moonlight. "That resembles a scene from *Rosemary's Babysitter*. Come on."

Crossing the graveyard, shadows stretched on the damp ground like a dark stain. My heart rate spiked, and I moved a little closer to Dax.

"You okay?" he asked softly.

"Yeah. Just a little spooked."

"Are you finally acknowledging the chilling allure of horror?"

"I'll have you know, sir, that the only chill I'm interested in involves ice cream and a heartwarming rom-com."

"Ah, but every good story has its moment of peril."

I brushed hair from my face. "Yes, but preferably less cemetery-ish."

The lampposts illuminated the walkways winding through the tombstones, statues, and crypts. Dax pushed open the heavy door.

My hand flew over my mouth. He had transformed the space with the glow of countless candles and a cozy picnic set up in the center of the room.

My eyes went wide. "Dax, what is all this?"

He grinned, shoving his hands into the pockets of his jeans. "Do you like it?"

A thick blanket and cushions were spread out on the ground, along with an assortment of delectable treats and fresh fruit.

Turning to face Dax, I whispered, "You did all this for me?"

He shrugged with a shy smile. "I wanted to do something special to show you how much I enjoy spending time with you. Especially since you're braving a creepy graveyard after reading a horror novel."

My laugh echoed off the stone walls. "Well, you certainly know how to make a girl feel special. Who needs dinner in a fancy restaurant when you can have a moonlit picnic surrounded by the dearly departed?"

"You get me like no one else, bookworm." Dax grasped my hand and led me to the blanket. "I figured if we're going to be friends long-term, we might as well hang out in a place that's as unique and unconventional as we are."

We relaxed among the flickering candlelight, and the closeness of Dax's presence enveloped me. I was having so much fun. In a graveyard. Inside a mausoleum.

And the weirdest thing? I was having a picnic with the man who had managed to make my pulse throb more times than I cared to admit. It was like a scene from a paranormal romance novel, and I couldn't suppress a laugh.

Dax quirked an eyebrow at me. "What's so funny?"

My mouth twitched. "Nothing, it's just...if you had

told me a few weeks ago I'd be having a candlelit date in a crypt, I would've laughed you out of my bookshop."

He opened the container of fruit and held it out to me. "I suppose life has a funny way of surprising us, huh?"

Plucking a grape, I popped it into my mouth. "It sure does. And do you know what? I wouldn't have it any other way."

A cool draft swept through the room. I shivered, rubbing my arms, the thin fabric of my sweater doing little to ward off the chill.

"Cold?" Dax edged closer.

"Maybe a little, but it's nothing a little body heat can't fix."

He gave me a sideways glance. "Is that Paris speak for 'cuddle with me'?"

My lips curved into a smile. "I prefer to think of it as a strategic sharing of resources. For survival purposes. Like a preemptive strike against the forces of hypothermia."

He scooted over until our sides were pressed firmly together. I laid my head against his shoulder. Above us, the night sky glittered through gaps in the old stone roof. We eased into silence, the kind that wasn't awkward but comfortable. His hand touched mine, tentative yet wanting, and when I threaded my fingers through his, it felt like the most natural thing in the world.

"Dax." I lifted my head to look at him. "You're becoming one of my best friends."

His expression clouded, then just as quickly, he forced a faint grin. "Um, yeah. You too, bookworm. This is the best non-date, date I've had in a long time."

"Oh, come on! Seriously?"

"I sorta stopped dating six months ago. On my last date, we spent the entire evening talking about her dog's digestive issues. I don't think I've ever learned so much about canine bowel movements in my life."

Grabbing a strawberry, I bit into it. "At least it was educational."

Dax raised an eyebrow. "I'm not sure that's the sort of riveting conversation I was looking for on a first date. What about you? I'm sure you've had your fair share of dating fails."

Unlacing our hands, I sat up. "Where do I even begin? One guy insisted on speaking in a British accent the entire night. Problem was, he kept slipping in and out of it. One minute he sounded like the Queen, the next he was straight out of Jersey Shore."

His forehead creased. "That's so weird! Did you ever figure out why he was doing it?"

"I was too afraid to ask. I just nodded along and tried not to crack up each time he said 'cheerio' or 'bloody hell'."

It felt so easy, so natural, to be here with Dax, trading stories and laughter under the starlit sky. I reached for a plump strawberry from the spread before us, my fingers brushing against his as he moved to do the same. My adrenaline did this crazy hormonal-pumping thing. I popped the fruit into my mouth, savoring its sweet tang.

Dax reclined on his elbows and studied me for a moment. "We've talked about a lot of things over the past month or so, bookworm, but I still feel like I barely know you. Tell me about your childhood."

"Growing up, my parents always made sure our house was filled with books. It was like living in a library but with snacks."

"Let me guess, your mom was the strict librarian type who shushed you for talking too loud?"

Reclining against the wall, I sighed. "Quite the opposite. Mom was a teacher, and she encouraged lively discussions about the books we read. Dad was the history buff. He'd launch into these long-winded lectures about the historical context of every novel."

"You had quite the literary upbringing. No wonder you ended up running a bookshop."

"It's in my blood, I suppose. Books have always been my constant companions, through thick and thin. They've taught me about love, life, and everything in between."

Dax turned to face me. "And what has the wise Paris Novak learned from all those books?"

"That life's unpredictable, messy, heartbreaking, and sometimes downright infuriating. But it's also beautiful, extraordinary, surprising...and fun."

"Spoken like a true romantic," he teased.

"I blame it on the Jane Austen novels I consumed as a teenager."

"Well, I may not be a Mr. Darcy, but I do have chivalrous manners." Dax cleared his throat and adopted a posh, exaggerated tone. "Miss Novak, would you do me the honor of reading your favorite scenes from *Rosemary's Babysitter*?"

I took the book from my purse. "Why, Mr. Granger, I thought you'd never ask."

Reading out loud, we discussed aspects of the book. I kept glancing at Dax, enjoying his company. He had somehow managed to slip past my defenses when I wasn't looking, leaving me equally giddy and terrified at the prospect of what that meant.

If someone had told me I'd soon be swoony over a muscle-bound beefcake allergic to romance novels, I'd have laughed in their face—but that was before Dax walked in and turned my bookish world upside down.

# Chapter Twelve

THE MOMENT I PUSHED OPEN THE CRAFT STORE door and entered Knit Wit, a whirl of colors and textures practically leaped off the shelves to greet me. Quilts hung on the walls, each one flaunting a pattern more complex than the last.

"Morning, Paris!" Mrs. Jeffreys stood behind the counter, her glasses perched precariously on the tip of her nose. "Here for more glitter?"

"Probably. I'm on a mission to create an eye-catching sign to advertise a sale in my bookshop. Any pipe cleaners?"

"Just got in a shipment that sparkles brighter than my grandkid's future." She pointed at aisle thirteen. "And you'll need googly eyes."

"Can't spell discount without a pair of oversized, life-like eyeballs." I gave her a conspiratorial smile, already envisioning my future masterpiece.

Mrs. Jeffreys chortled, shaking her head. "Well, if anyone can pull off an advertisement with googly eyes, it's you. How are you doing?"

"Thriving on book matching and pastries, as usual." I

pushed a lock of lavender hair out of my face. "I have high hopes this sign will lure in the skeptics who think 'book club' is code for 'cult.'"

"Ah, those poor, ignorant souls. Let me know if you need any help finding anything."

I sauntered off toward the paint aisle, leaving no craft supply unturned in my quest for signage supremacy.

While scrutinizing a flamboyant shade of pink glitter paint and debating its potential to convey 'irresistible book sale,' the door opened.

Dax waltzed inside in a muscle tank and destroyed my Zen. My heart executed a clumsy somersault. His light-brown hair was ruffled as if he'd wrestled with a particularly frisky breeze on the way over.

Our eyes met, and we exchanged shy smiles.

"We seem to have a knack for bumping into each other in the most unexpected places." I really hoped my voice sounded blasé and not like I'd just inhaled helium.

"It's like we live in a small town," Dax joked. "Should we plan a serendipitous meeting at the grocery store next?"

"Knowing our luck, probably a run-in at the town's annual pie-eating contest."

"I'll be sure to wear my stretchy pants. But hey, I'm not complaining."

"Yeah, me neither." I shuffled my feet. "What're you doing here?"

He wore a lopsided smile. "Just thought I'd try to learn glass etching. I need a new hobby." His voice had a warm, rumbly quality.

"Look at you, going all Renaissance man on me. What's next, blacksmithing on your days off?"

He rubbed his chin. "I'd rather take up quilting. Make blankets inscribed with quotes from Edgar Allan Poe."

I grinned. "Ah, a niche market just ripe for the taking."

The idea of Dax, with his well-toned personal trainer physique, sitting around stitching *Nevermore* onto a quilt was oddly endearing.

He jerked his chin toward the explosion of crafting supplies in the basket near my feet. "What's the haul for? Another visual assault on the citizens of Bluebell Bend?"

"Assault is such a strong word. I prefer 'aggressive invitation to reading.'" I made air quotes with my fingers, then lowered my arms. "I'm creating a sign for a book sale next week."

Dax nodded. "So, you're about to unleash a glitter bomb of literary proportions. If anyone can make reading irresistible, it's you, bookworm."

"I might just have to pencil you in as my plus-one for the book sale. Just for moral support and eye-candy."

We laughed. I sensed the attraction ramping up between us—or it was just the residual fumes from the paint aisle.

As Dax crouched to grasp an etching kit on a lower shelf, an eReader made an insidious escape from his jacket pocket, taking a nosedive onto the floor with a soft thud. I glowered at the device—not from the impact, but from what it represented.

The sight of that electronic book imposter sent a twinge of repulsion through me. I had always been on team physical books. I loved turning the crisp pages and inhaling the fragrance of ink and paper that an eReader could never replicate.

Dax dropped to one knee with the swiftness of someone used to squatting heavy weights, his face flushing a shade that matched the burgundy yarn on the nearest display. When he straightened, eReader in hand, he shot me a sheepish grin.

"I'm a secret book hoarder," he said, brushing off the device.

The aisle thickened with friction that felt uncomfortably close to a book club debate gone south. My fingers itched for the calming feel of a paperback to show my print-only allegiance. In life I had two rules: never fall for a Kindle-wielding scoundrel—especially if he had swoon-worthy biceps, and don't ever start a conga line at a funeral —*don't ask.*

"*Ugh.* Just when I was starting to like you!" I shot his traitorous contraband a look that could curdle ink. "Why an eReader? I feel like I don't know you at all! Next thing I know, you'll be revealing your passion for taxidermy."

Dax, unfazed, waggled the device at me. "This little gadget holds an entire library. Can your bookshelves do that without collapsing?"

This called for immediate intervention. Dax might be easy on the eyes, but I wasn't giving in that easily.

My brows arched in mock superiority. "There's an intimacy in flipping through pages, you know. An appeal that your cold, lifeless screen could never hope to capture."

"*Please,* it's practical. And how very closed-minded of you, bookworm." He tapped the eReader gently against his palm and drew back his shoulders. "Seems to me like someone's stuck in the past. You have heard of evolution?"

A scoff escaped me and I stepped back to regain some fragment of high ground amidst aisles of crafting supplies. "*Ha!* More like a digital devolution. I'll stick with actual books, thank you very much. They may be old-fashioned, but at least I don't need a charger to turn the page."

Dax's stiff posture relaxed, his argumentative fire

dimming to embers. "Maybe so, but it's the love of reading that counts, right?"

His logic hit me like a well-aimed hardcover. As much as I hated to admit it, Dax had a point. Our bickering, though spirited, was just the surface of our favorite pastime—a shared love for stories, however, they were consumed.

"No, um, eReader can compete with the smell and feel of a well-worn paperback in your hands."

He shook his head. "You're cute."

I frowned. "Don't change the subject."

"I'm not. Just stating facts. You're adorable when you're passionate about something, even if it's your undying love for dead trees and ink stains."

Unable to maintain my stern expression, I fought a smile. Something about Dax's tenacity made it impossible to stay annoyed with him for long. Like trying to hold a grudge against a puppy—an absurdly handsome puppy with a talent for pushing my buttons.

"You're hopeless, Dax. I suppose that's part of your infuriating charm."

Dax gave a casual shrug. "Honestly, if I read an eBook and it really grabs me, I buy a physical copy. It's the best of both worlds And I don't mind paying for it twice."

I tilted my head. "That's so sweet, in a nerdy, book-loving sort of way. And I see your point, but I still maintain there's something magical about holding a physical book in your hands." I shuffled back a step, my foot bumping my basket. "I know we have our different tastes when it comes to reading material and how we consume our stories, so for now, I guess we'll just have to agree to disagree."

Dax's grin only widened in that unfairly attractive way of his. "That's a diplomatic way to put it."

"Because I'm a master of tact and grace." I gave him a

curtsy, nearly knocking over a display of embroidery hoops in the process.

"Grace, huh?" His laugh was a sound I'd bottle if I could—rich and luxurious.

My ears burned. "Oh, shut up."

We both smiled.

"You're impossible, bookworm. Your love of reading is as charming as it is stubborn. One day you'll have to let me show you the merits of the digital side, and maybe we can find a middle ground between your books and my convenient swipes."

His proximity was unsettling, causing my heart to do a little cha-cha in my chest. "Don't hold your breath, eReader boy."

We started wandering the aisles of the craft store.

Dax reached for a pack of multicolored, glitter pens. "These would be perfect for your sign. Just remember, with great glitter comes great responsibility."

Snatching the pens from his hand, I snorted. "I think I can handle it, but thanks for the vote of confidence." I shook my head. "You're ridiculous, you know that?"

He gave me a cute, crooked smile. "Ridiculously charming, you mean?"

"More like ridiculously determined to distract me from my crafting mission. Don't you have some weights to lift or a treadmill to conquer?"

Dax crossed his arms. "And miss out on the joy of watching you bedazzle? Not a chance."

"Oh, stop it. Next, you'll be telling me you secretly enjoy knitting sweaters for kittens."

Dax took a step closer. "There's a lot you don't know about me, but I'd love the chance to show you."

Damn him and his adorableness. He was somehow

managing to pierce the armor I'd protectively constructed around my heart. For a second, I allowed myself to imagine what it might be like to let someone in, to share my world with a man who wasn't confined to the pages of a book.

Then those insidious doubts and fears crept over me, causing an ache in my chest, a dull throb that pulsed in time with my heartbeat. Ever since Julian had broken my heart, I found myself putting up walls, trying to protect myself from getting hurt like that again. It was my way of shielding myself from any future disappointments. Yet even as I hid behind those walls, a part of me still longed for that connection, for someone to really understand me. The thought of trusting again, though? That was just too scary to even consider.

With a salute, he said, "I need to find stencils. Be right back."

Reaching for a glue gun, I saw it. My heart rate tripled. Lurking in the corner of the shelf was a massive black spider, its spindly legs poised for attack. I let out a yelp, and jumped back nearly rear-ending a display of washi tape in my haste to get away.

"Dax!" My voice rose a few octaves higher than usual. "*Help!*"

Dax emerged from around the corner. "What's wrong?"

I pointed a shaky finger at the eight-legged monstrosity. "Spider. P-please get rid of it."

His eyes widened when he spotted the creature, clearly sympathetic to my display of arachnophobia.

"Whoa, that's a big one. Okay, stay calm. I've got this."

Dax grabbed a nearby craft magazine, gently coaxing the spider onto the glossy cover. I was equal parts horrified and impressed, as he carefully carried the offending arachnid to the front door and released it outside.

"There you go, little guy. Find a new home, preferably far away from here." He stepped back inside and shut the door.

My body sagged against the wall. "I don't know what I would've done if you weren't here."

Dax dusted off his hands. "Probably screamed bloody murder and scared away all the customers. You might've even been banned from the craft store."

"Hey, I resent that!" I laughed, lightly swatting his arm. "I'll have you know I'm perfectly capable of handling a spider crisis...as long as it's from a safe distance and involves a lot of dramatic shrieking."

"Quite the team we make, huh? The bookworm and the arachnid-whisperer."

It was true—we did make a good team. I gave his hand a quick squeeze as a gesture of gratitude and camaraderie. The touch of his skin sent a warm prickling up my arm, and I quickly pulled away, hoping he hadn't noticed my lusty reaction.

We made our way to the checkout counter. A sense of contentment settled over me from the ease of our friendship. Even if we didn't agree on everything, there was something undeniably special about our relationship. And I wasn't just saying that because he saved me from a spider.

# Chapter Thirteen

I dawdled after work at The Grind House, a local coffee shop. I was surrounded by the scent of freshly roasted coffee beans and the hum of quiet conversations. Sunlight streamed through the windows, gleaming on the tables and chairs. I relaxed into a seat by the window, my steaming cappuccino in one hand and my phone in the other.

Sipping my drink, I scrolled through the comments on my latest bookstagram post, grinning at the flurry of notifications that lit up my screen. My followers were engaging in spirited discussions about the horror reading challenge I had thrown their way. It was a departure from our usual romance fare, but it still seemed to resonate with the bookish community.

I read the comments with a big, goofy smile.

*Ohhh, I've never been a horror fan, but your post has convinced me to give it a try!* one comment read.

*Anyone else super impressed with Paris's versatility in genres? I'm always excited to see what she posts next,* another commented.

*Count me in for the scary reads! Paris, you're turning me into a book nerd for life!* declared a third.

Reading their comments, my heart expanded. When I first started my bookstagram account, I never imagined how it would take on a life of its own, connecting me with people across the globe who shared my passion for reading.

"Hey, Paris!" Rachel called out.

Lowering my phone, I looked up at my best friend meandering over to my table. "You wouldn't believe the responses that I've been getting for the new horror reading challenge."

"That's fantastic. It's great to see you inspiring so many others." My bestie slid into the seat across from me, reached over, and then took a sip of my cappuccino.

I smiled. "I always wanted to be a book influencer."

Rachel drummed her fingertips on the table. "Sooo, I've been hearing some interesting buzz around town. Rumor has it that a certain fitness guru has been monopolizing a lot of your time lately. What's the story with you and Dax?"

At the mention of his name, I stared into the remnants of the foam floating in my cup. Our friendship had come to mean a lot to me in such a short time. And trying to keep my feelings for Dax in check was like attempting to herd cats while wearing catnip perfume—an exercise in futility and potential scratches.

Wrapping my hands around my mug, I took a deep breath. "Rachel, I'm just... scared," I admitted, my voice cracking with emotion. "You know I've been hurt before, and I've built walls. High ones."

The admission sat heavily on my tongue, each syllable carrying the baggage of my past heartbreaks and the angst still gripping my heart.

She gave me a soft smile. "It's natural to want to protect

your heart. But sometimes, the most worthwhile things in life require us to be a little brave and vulnerable. Dax isn't like those other guys who hurt you. I know him, he's caring and considerate."

Fidgeting with the napkin, I tore at it, tiny shreds littering the table. "What if we crash and burn? I don't want to lose him. Not as a friend."

Rachel placed a hand over mine, stilling my restless fingers. "Consider what you're gaining, not losing. And think about it this way—if your friendship with Dax is already strong, even if a romantic relationship didn't work out, that foundation would still be there."

Since Dax had joined the book club, I pondered the crazy turns my life had taken. He had somehow managed to wiggle his way into my life when I wasn't looking, and I had sorely misjudged him. The truth was, I liked him a lot. It was the little things he did, like saving me from spiders or surprising me with a graveyard picnic that made me realize just how much he cared. Dax had a way of making me feel special too, as if I was the only person in the world that mattered.

And it wasn't just his considerate side I found adorable, Dax was also the most reliable person I had ever met. I knew I could count on him to be there, no matter what. He had become one of my closest friends.

Taking the last sip of my now tepid cappuccino, my turmoil settled like sediment at the bottom of the cup. "You've given me a lot to think about."

Rachel glanced at my empty mug. "How about a refill?"

"Sure, make mine with a double shot of bravery, would you?" I handed her my cup.

She walked to the counter and returned moments later with two steaming mugs. Rachel retook her seat. "Here you go, extra courage for my favorite bookstagrammer. Look, I know you're unsure, but I'm team Dax if it makes your decision any easier."

I let out a long exhale. The attraction between Dax and me was genuine and extended beyond the physical. Some of our late night conversations had stretched into the early morning hours, and the threads of our lives had become more intricately entwined.

"I'm just so afraid of getting hurt again."

She touched my arm. "It seems like Dax cares about you, and you deserve to be loved fully for who you are. Because you're awesome, hon."

My throat tightened. If I wanted to move forward, I had to confront the fears holding me back.

I fidgeted, my finger tracing the delicate swirls painted on the ceramic cup. "Dax is...he's so certain about what he wants. And me? I'm all over the place, like a bookmark lost between pages," I said, raising my voice over the hiss of the espresso machine. "Every time I think I know where I'm going, I hit a dead end of doubt."

My thoughts shifted to that cheater, Julian. His betrayal had left a scar on my soul that just wouldn't fade, no matter how much time passed. Whenever I closed my eyes, I could still see his face. Even those once trusting eyes that had looked at me with such affection, but turned cold and distant in the end. My chest hurt. It was like an invisible hand was squeezing the air out of my lungs every time I thought about it. Finding out about Julian's engagement to another woman completely shattered the future I'd imagined for us. And deep down, I knew Dax was different, but I couldn't fully trust again without risking another heartbreak.

Rachel squeezed my arm, her grip grounding me in the

moment. "Even when you feel lost, trust that your heart's guiding you to where you're meant to be."

She always knew how to make me see the lighter side of things, even when I was caught up in my own overthinking.

"If only it were that easy." I sighed.

"Hey, there's no hurry. You'll find your way when you're ready."

My chest expanded with a rush of gratitude for my best friend. The cafe buzzed around us, clinking dishes and muffled conversations.

"No matter what happens, I'll be here. Literary Persuasions stick together, right?"

"Right..." I sniffled, the knot in my chest loosening.

The door opened and in strode Samuel, Aunt Margo, and Carmen. They ordered drinks and then joined us at nearby tables, with a steaming mug of coffee or tea cradled in their hands.

My forehead scrunched and I looked at my best friend. "Did you invite the book club?"

Rachel shrugged. "A new venue for our monthly meeting."

"Paris, honey, I feel the stars aligning today. With Mars and Jupiter in such a fortuitous arrangement, you're destined for a year of surprising romantic encounters," Aunt Margo said. "Your soulmate could be orchestrated by the celestial powers that be!" My aunt's arms swept through the air with the fervor of an oracle.

But one errant gesture came too close to her iced latte. The cup wobbled ominously before toppling over, sending a flood of chilled coffee rushing across the surface.

Pushing back my chair, I scrambled to my feet. "Oh, no."

Rachel spun in her chair, her movements quick but

disastrously miscalculated. In a reflex of self-preservation, her hand flung her steaming latte into the air like a hot, caffeinated grenade. The cup arced through the air before its contents splattered on Samuel's lap.

He jumped up with a yelp, his chair clattering to the ground behind him. The noise and commotion drew the attention of every patron, and the coffee shop erupted into gasps and stifled giggles.

Aunt Margo, blissfully undeterred by the pandemonium she'd orchestrated, simply dabbed at a coffee splash on her scarf. "Oops."

Everybody retook their seats while a barista mopped up the table.

Turning to Samuel, a sympathetic grimace crossed my face. "Are you okay? That looked like a *latte* of trouble."

Samuel retrieved his chair and brushed off his pants. "Quite all right. No need to cry over spilled coffee."

"Next time, let's stick to less volatile subjects—like a quiet discussion on poetry?" Leaning back, my mismatched socks peeked out from under the hem of my jeans and made me think of Dax and me doing laundry together. "Since we're all here, I've been thinking about this month's theme for the club."

"What do you suggest?" Samuel asked.

Carmen held her mug, blowing on the top to cool it. "As an artist, I'm all for exploring new perspectives."

"I was thinking we could dive into the world of Jane Austen, specifically *Emma*. There's just something about her witty humor and social commentary. And it's practically a manual on how *not* to matchmake in a small town." I pointedly looked at my aunt.

Rachel raised an eyebrow. "Does this have anything to

do with your reading challenge with Dax? How's that going?"

"Surprisingly well." I took a sip of my coffee, savoring the taste. "He's actually reading *Emma* now and I thought we could join him."

Carmen tilted her head. "*Ah.* The original meddling matchmaker. I can see the appeal. Reading about Emma blundering her way through love could teach us all a thing or two."

Samuel drank his black coffee. "I believe there's a certain charm to Austen's writing, even if it is somewhat frivolous for my tastes."

I sat up. "I'll have you know that *Emma* is a masterpiece of social satire and character development."

Aunt Margo fluffed her hair, her turquoise jewelry jangling. "Yes, and I'm eager to debate whether Mr. Knightley is the unsung hero or just another gentleman bystander."

Drinking the last of my coffee, I placed the mug on the table. "I vote unsung hero. Anyone who can handle Emma's scheming with such patience deserves a medal—or at least a strong cup of coffee."

Rachel sighed. "And let's not forget about poor Harriet Smith. That girl got tossed around like a salad at one of those overly enthusiastic brunch spots."

"I always did love a good romance. And the way Austen skewers the upper crust of society? Delightful!" Aunt Margo said.

Carmen bobbed her head. "Count me in, *querida*. I'm always up for a good discussion on the foibles of the human heart."

"Then it's settled," I said. "We'll all read *Emma* and meet again to discuss the book."

As the conversation wrapped up, a surge of gratitude for this extraordinary group of individuals who had become my literary lifeline in Bluebell Bend struck me. While I may have always felt like the odd bookworm in this quaint little town, my fellow book club members never failed to make me feel understood and appreciated.

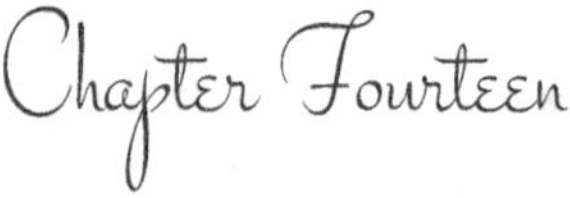

*Dax*

GHOSTLY SHADOWS SLUNK ON THE WALLS, thanks to the candles strategically placed in my living room. The dim lighting created menacing silhouettes of the fake cobwebs and paper bats strung from the ceiling and arches. The plastic skull on the coffee table grinned back at me.

The couches were pushed together, creating an impromptu movie theater, and every seat faced the large flat-screen TV mounted on the wall. I wrestled with the popcorn machine, ensuring it was primed to pump out enough buttery popcorn to feed the group.

Tonight wasn't just about entertaining the Literary Persuasion Society; it was about Paris and me, and showing her I could be a part of her inner-circle.

*Just a movie night with friends...and the woman you can't stop thinking about.*

My chosen lineup of horror flicks, spanning from Hitchcock's iconic scares to contemporary hits, were stacked on the table. The plan was not only to match everyone's horror palette but also gently introduce Paris to my world without sending her sprinting for the hills.

The doorbell rang. Samuel and Rachel strode inside and seemed impressed by the spooky decorations.

"Welcome to fright night!" I greeted.

Rachel slipped off her sweater. "Dax, this setup is killer!"

"Simply stupendous," Samuel said.

"I appreciate that." I slid the first film into the DVD player.

Rachel sat on the couch. "William was gonna come too, but he has a sore throat. Which means more popcorn for me."

"That's, uh, cool." I was trying to appear nonchalant while keeping an eye on the door.

A few minutes later, Paris entered my home, looking gorgeous in a snug tee, ripped jeans, and high-top sneakers. Her perfume held a trace of peach blossoms and floral notes that made my heartbeat accelerate.

She set her purse and jacket on the table. "Aunt Margo and Carmen can't make it tonight, their at a pottery class."

"All right, folks." I clapped my hands for attention. "Let's get this movie marathon started. Remember, it's all fun and games until someone ends up possessed." I grabbed the remote and kicked off the first movie.

Rachel, contentedly ensconced with a bowl of popcorn on her lap, tapped the cushion next to her, signaling Paris to join. Samuel sank into the other leather sofa. Paris sat beside Rachel, and I took a seat beside her—close enough to exchange quiet comments while giving her enough room to breathe.

Every jump scare was punctuated by Paris's quick intake of breath. Her hands would occasionally graze mine when she reached for the popcorn, causing a fierce tremor in my heart's rhythm.

"Is it just me or does the killer have a striking resemblance to Mr. Jenkins from the grocery store?" Samuel said, adjusting his spectacles.

Rachel hugged a throw pillow to her chest, her knuckles turning white. "Maybe he has a secret night job at the morgue that we don't know about."

The chilling score intensified, heralding the killer's imminent strike. I leaned in, shoveling popcorn into my mouth.

Rachel lifted the pillow. "I can't watch," she whimpered, burying her face in the fabric.

The movies were great, yet I kept sneaking glances at Paris. It always struck me as odd that she could be tagged as an outcast by others around town, ridiculed for all the cute ways she stood apart. However, she never let anyone's harsh judgment bend her spirit. She stayed true to herself, undeterred, and never once stooped to unkindness. That strength, that grace under pressure, only deepened my admiration—and my feelings—for her.

Hours later the credits rolled on the last film of the night.

Rachel stood up. "Thanks, Dax. This was fun."

"Certainly more exciting than my usual Friday nights," Samuel said.

Samuel and Rachel walked to the door. They offered their thanks once more before heading out into the night, leaving me and Paris alone.

"Can you stay?" I sat near her on the leather couch.

Paris frowned. "Sure. Everything okay?"

"Yeah. I just..." I rubbed the back of my neck. "I wanted to talk to you."

"What's up?"

Damn, there was so much I liked about this girl. Where should I start? How to let her know how I feel?

I cleared my throat. "I just wanted to tell you...that one thing I really like about you is your sense of humor. It's sharp, quirky. And the way you throw a joke into the mix? Makes every conversation a little livelier, a little smarter."

Paris grinned. "Aw, shucks. Why am I getting all this praise?"

"Because I've met so many women who seem to only care about superficial things, you know? Chasing after guys for their looks or their bank accounts, putting on an act to be someone they think I want them to be. It's all so fake and exhausting. What I'm looking for is someone genuine. I want a connection that goes beyond just looks. It's the substance that matters to me, the real person underneath it all." I stood back up and shoved my hands into my pockets. "In a town where everyone seems to follow the same script, you're writing your own. That's real. And I respect that a lot."

And that's exactly why Paris stood out—she was the real deal, didn't put on airs, and that sincerity had pulled me in.

"That's so sweet." Her cheeks tinged a soft pink. "I had fun tonight. I was sorta hesitant about watching those scary movies, but I ended up really enjoying them. Guess you're slowly converting me to expand my genre likes."

"Then my mission's accomplished," I replied with a grin.

She rubbed her stomach. "I should go. I haven't eaten much today."

"No, stay. Are you craving a late night snack? The kitchen's through there."

We made our way into the kitchen. The stainless steel appliances gleamed under the recessed lighting. Paris made a beeline for the fridge.

"All right, Dax, let's see what you've got." She rummaged through the shelves. "Kale, spinach, tofu..." She looked at me. "Where's the real food?"

I chuckled. "That *is* real food, Paris. Essential nutrients for the body."

"Fuel for the soul is what I need. Like...*Aha!*" She emerged with a pint of Ben & Jerry's. "Now we're talking."

"Ice cream? At this hour?"

"It's always ice cream o'clock somewhere." She opened a drawer and grabbed a spoon.

"Must be left over from the last time my brother visited."

"What's your favorite flavor?"

"I'm more of a smoothie guy. Blend up protein powder, almond milk, throw in a banana..."

Paris wrinkled her nose. "*Boring.* You need to live a little. Expand your culinary palate."

"Hey, I can get wild in the kitchen. You should try my famous grilled chicken and quinoa salad."

She snorted. "Sounds yummy, but that's *not* wild."

I inclined against the counter, crossing my arms. "All right, bookworm, what's your idea of a gourmet meal?"

"Easy. Peanut butter and jelly sandwich, but with the crusts cut off. Gourmet yum."

I laughed. "Wow, that's some Michelin-star level cuisine right there."

She dug into the pint of ice cream. "I do enjoy baking. There's something therapeutic about it."

I watched her savor another spoonful, her pink lips

closing around the utensil. Damn, even the way she ate ice cream was sexy.

"So aside from elite sandwich-making, any other talents I should know about?"

"Chocolate chip cookies. The secret is in the brown butter. Takes them to a whole new level."

"I'll have to try them sometime."

She gave me a coy look. "Play your cards right, and I'll bake you a batch."

Oh, I'd play any hand she dealt me. Paris Novak, with her snarky humor and unrepentant love for all things sugary, had me completely smitten. This night was shaping up to be sweeter than I'd imagined. Especially when it involved quality time with a certain beautiful woman. She was one craving I didn't plan on denying myself.

Paris dug the spoon into the pint with gusto. She gestured at me with the loaded utensil. "This right here? The ultimate comfort food." She popped the bite into her mouth, closing her eyes in blissful appreciation. "Mmm, sweet, creamy, indulgent. Everything your boring healthy meals aren't."

"I never said my meals were exciting. At least they're fueling my body right, not just satisfying a sugar craving."

She scooped up another spoonful of ice cream and held it out to me. "Here, live a little. Embrace the decadence."

I hesitated. One bite wouldn't kill me, but it was a slippery slope. Next thing I knew, I'd be scarfing down entire pints of Rocky Road while binge-watching rom-coms and ditching my morning runs.

"Come on, Dax," she cooed. "Don't be so rigid."

Was that how she really saw me? Some inflexible, by-the-book guy? If so, no wonder she didn't view me as dating material. I prided myself on my easygoing personality, but maybe I came across as too nitpicky, too predictable. Well, if that was the case, I aimed to change her perception tonight.

She stepped closer until the spoon hovered temptingly near my mouth. The cloying chocolate aroma wafted my way, and I had to admit it smelled damn tempting. Could I let one indulgent bite derail my disciplined diet?

"Just a taste." Paris's lips curved into a sexy smile as if she could read the war waging inside me.

Ah, screw it. If indulging her sweet tooth meant getting closer to Paris, sign me up for a cavity.

Never breaking eye contact, I leaned in and closed my mouth around the spoon. The burst of cold sweetness on my tongue made me groan. "Okay, damn. That's good."

Her lips curved upward into a slow, satisfied smile. "Now was that so bad?"

"No..." I licked a stray bit of chocolate from the corner of my mouth.

She busied herself rinsing the spoon, her back to me. I hopped onto the island counter, admiring her beautiful lavender hair. The urge to hold her in my arms and breathe in her skin was overwhelming.

"Now that I know your diet preferences..." I cocked my head, studying her. "Tell me, Miss Prose and Positivity, what's your grand philosophy on life?"

"Getting deep now, are we?" She tapped a finger against her chin. "I believe in living authentically. Embracing your true self. Why live any other way?"

"I hear you. But easier said than done, right? Society's always pushing us to fit in neat little boxes."

Paris snorted. "Oh, I know. It's like, I love running my bookshop and geeking out over Jane Austen. I'm also the weirdo who dyes her hair purple and exists on Pop-Tarts."

"Hey, I'm right there with you. Personal trainer by day,

horror junkie by night. My Stephen King obsession isn't exactly prime dinner conversation."

"Um, says who? That's exactly the kind of dinner chat I'm here for!" She reclined against the sink. "So, big guy, what's your philosophy on life?"

"For me, it's about resilience. I believe in rolling with the punches. Life knocks you down, you get back up. Not with bitterness, but by moving forward, always forward."

"Resilience. I like that." Paris tilted her head, lavender strands brushing her cheek. "Not letting life keep you down."

Jumping off the counter, I closed the distance between us. "It's about balance. And building real connections. That's why this—" I gestured between us— "matters to me."

Her breath hitched. "Wow, that's profound. And here I thought you were all about fun and the flippant remarks."

"I can be serious, too. Particularly about things—and the people—I care about." I hoped she caught the deeper implication. "Don't get me wrong, finding joy in the little things is also part of a good philosophy."

Paris folded her arms, her gaze thoughtful. "You're quite the philosopher. It's so..."

"Unexpected?" I quirked a brow. "What can I say? I contain multitudes."

A laugh burst from her lips, bright and infectious. "Quoting Walt Whitman? Be still my beating heart."

I winked. "See? I'm not just a dumb jock."

She swatted my chest. "I never thought that. Okay, maybe for, like, a second, but I'm officially revising that assessment."

We stood there, gazes locked, the air between us electric. Her scent, vanilla and peachy shampoo, filled my head. I wanted to pull her close, taste her lips, yet I held back. This thing between us was special.

"So," I said softly, "still think I'm not your type?"

Pink tinged her cheeks. "You're certainly not who I thought you were."

"I hope that's a good thing."

"It is..." She smiled. "It definitely is."

My heart soared. At that moment, I knew I was a goner. This brilliant, beautiful, hardheaded woman saw me, the real me. And she liked what she saw.

*Just spit it out already.*

I wiped my sweaty palms on my jeans. "I need to tell you something..."

"Whatever it is, you can say it."

Clearing my throat, I blurted, "I...I'm falling for you. *Hard.*" The words tumbled out in a rush. "Everything just clicks when you're around, in a way it never has before."

She opened her mouth, but I held up a hand.

"Wait, let me get this out before I lose my nerve." I sucked in a deep breath, letting it whoosh out. "Look, I might not be the most successful or intellectual guy, but I care about you, Paris. More than I've ever cared for anyone. I need to know if you feel this thing between us too. Or am I just fooling myself here?"

"Dax..." Paris bit her lip, glancing away. "I have feelings for you too, and you're a great guy. You're one of my closest friends and I don't want to screw that up."

My stomach dropped into my trainers. Rejection stung like a punch to the gut...and damn it hurt.

"I don't get it. What's holding you back, what's got you so scared?" I wanted to pry those reasons out of her, to understand what made her hesitant.

She sighed. "A lot of reasons. Maybe because in almost

every romance, the second you let your guard down, the universe conspires to make you regret it."

I huffed out a tense chuckle. "Should I be worried about grand gestures and airport chases?"

"Only if you plan on leaving the country without telling me." She ducked her head and her long hair hid her face.

I reached out to tuck the silky strands behind her ear, my fingers grazing her cheek. "Paris, you know I'd never hurt you."

She leaned into my touch for a fleeting second before pulling back. "I want to believe you, but..." She shook her head. "Guys always say that and then they change their minds."

"I'm not like other guys." I tipped her chin up, willing her to see the sincerity in my eyes. "When I commit to someone, I'm all in. No games, no lies."

"Sounds like you're auditioning to be the next *Bachelor*," she teased. "All you're missing is the rose and the dramatic music swelling in the background."

"Listen..." I said, pausing to find the right words. "I can't guarantee life won't throw us a few curves, and sure, we're as different as a kettlebell and a bookmark. Different genres, different views...but that's exactly why we're so good together."

She stepped back, putting distance between us. "I've been down this road before. Falling for someone who seems perfect, only to have it all crumble. I'm not sure I'm brave enough to risk that again."

"It's okay," I said gently. "We don't have to figure it all out now. And I meant what I said before, I like spending time with you."

She let out a shaky breath. "I like spending time with you too, but..."

The last thing I wanted was for Paris to feel pressured.

"I get it," I replied immediately. "You don't have to say anything else."

She turned and walked away.

Once the door closed behind her, the energy in the room seemed to vanish with her. Disappointment sank heavily on me as I took down the decorations.

Paris had her doubts, but she hadn't given me a flat no. That ambiguity held a thread of hope. I wouldn't push her into making a decision about us, but somehow, I had to prove that whatever fears were holding her back could be overcome.

After stowing the last of the Halloween gear, I sprawled out on the couch. A copy of *Emma*—the last book in the genre swap—sat on the coffee table and I snatched it up.

There had to be a way to get Paris to change her mind or at least give us a chance. She was obviously attracted to me and we had this off-the-charts chemistry. My gut told me we were meant for something great. I just needed to figure out how to prove it to her, how to break through her reservations.

Cracking the spine, I knew one thing for certain—I wasn't ready to give up on Paris just yet.

# Chapter Fifteen

A FEW WEEKS HAD PASSED SINCE THE BOOK CLUB had started reading *Emma*, and today I was embracing the spirit of the era.

Enjoying the bright sunshine, I twirled in my elegant Regency-era gown, the delicate muslin fabric billowing around me in a soft pastel shade. The high empire-waistline and short puffed sleeves embodied the simplicity and grace of the early 18th-century fashion, while the modest neckline added a trace of refinement.

The crisp wind tousled my hair as I draped the final blanket over the grass, stepping back to admire my handiwork. The charming scene looked like it had sprung straight from the pages of a Jane Austen novel as if the renowned author herself had RSVP'd to my garden party.

"Paris, you've outdone yourself." Aunt Margo, in a bonnet festooned with ribbons, glided towards me. She donned a chemise dress made of thin, white muslin with a sash tied around her waist. "It's like we've been transported straight to Regency England!"

Intent on recreating the realism of the period, I had

spread out two large blankets. On serving trays I placed cold roasted meats, fruit pastries, bread, and cheese. Paper lanterns hung from the trees and soft classical music played from a discreetly placed Bluetooth speaker.

"Thank you, Aunt Margo. You look great."

"Paris, this is spectacular. Just like the scene from *Emma*." Samuel ambled over, his waistcoat impeccably tailored to accommodate his portly stature. "This feels even more authentic than my spreadsheets."

"Your cravat alone deserves its own ledger entry, Samuel. *Bravo!*" I applauded his attention to detail.

"Bonjour." Rachel's voice sang out, arriving in a pretty gown of light-pink. Her onyx curls had been tamed into an elegant updo. She carried a basket bursting with what I knew would be baked goods capable of making Mr. Darcy himself weak at the knees.

"Rachel, you look like you've stepped straight out of a French romance novel." I beamed, already angling for a macaron.

Rachel handed me a pastry with a smile so warm it could soften butter. "This is the best Literary Persuasion Society meeting yet."

Settling on the edge of the blanket, I surveyed the park, the manicured lawn dotted with clusters of flowers and towering oak trees. The aroma of blooming honeysuckle vines and the subtle sweetness of lavender wafted through the air. Squirrels darted among the branches, their chattering melding with the distant laughter of children on the playground equipment.

"Hello, hello, everyone." Carmen arrived last, her tall frame wrapped in a long dress of deep burgundy velvet that complimented her dark hair and kind eyes. A colorful shawl was draped around her shoulders. "Paris, *querida*, this setting is a living painting."

"I was going for 'Jane Austen meets Bluebell Bend.' Do you think I nailed it?" I asked, hoping for her artistic stamp of approval.

"Indubitably, *querida*," she said with a graceful nod. "Where is Dax? Will he be joining us today?"

All eyes fixed on me.

"Um, yeah. I sent him a text yesterday and he said he'd be here after work," I said.

"All right, everyone, grab a glass of lemonade. Let's toast to an afternoon of delightful company and literary debate." Samuel smiled, lifting his drink.

Aunt Margo waved a hand adorned with an assortment of gemstone rings. "And here's to Paris, for bringing Austen to life in the park."

Everybody cheered, our laughter merging with the distant chirp of birdsong.

"Now, let's discuss Emma's matchmaking skills or lack thereof," Samuel said, grabbing a cold cut.

Just as our discussion was gaining momentum, I caught sight of Dax. He strolled up the path, looking as dashing as Mr. Knightley himself. My breath caught at the sight of him in fitted breeches, polished boots, and a tailcoat accentuating his athletic build.

I had to remind myself to breathe. "Mr. Knightley, I presume?"

He gave me a roguish grin. "The very same, Miss Woodhouse," he replied with a sweeping bow. "This gathering of yours puts *Downton Abbey* to shame."

The compliment made me smile. "I'm glad you could join us. What did you think of *Emma*?"

Dax's expression turned thoughtful. "At first I struggled to relate to a matchmaking heroine and provincial village life. But your passion for Austen inspired me to keep an open mind. By the end of the story, I was invested in the characters and their happily-ever-afters." He licked his lips. "What I'm saying is, I feel like romance and horror aren't so different after all. They both have the power to evoke strong emotions and keep you turning the pages late into the night."

Dax's appreciation for the romance genre affected me deeply. It was like finding a unicorn—a man who not only tolerated my love for all things swoony and heartfelt but actually embraced it. Most guys wouldn't sit through a discussion on the merits of Mr. Knightley's character development much less dress like him. It was enough to make a bookish girl's heart skip a beat.

The book club chatted about the storyline, losing ourselves in an animated discussion of its themes of self-discovery, gender roles, and romance. Next, we debated Emma's faults and Mr. Knightley's merits while nibbling on the food.

"Emma was such a busybody." Aunt Margo fanned herself with a hand-painted fan. "All that prying into other people's love lives...I'd have just consulted their star charts. Much more efficient."

Samuel tugged at the hem of his intricately embroidered waistcoat. "There's something to be said for the thrill of the chase, even if the stars have already spelled it out."

Rachel shifted her position on the blanket. "Thrill or no thrill, I'd rather not have my future dictated by celestial bodies."

I nodded. "And I'd rather hold out for a love story like Emma and Mr. Knightley's—full of surprises."

Carmen patted Dax's shoulder. "As I recall, Dax was

quite the skeptic about romance novels, weren't you? And now look at you, all dapper and debating Jane Austen."

All heads turned towards Dax, who shrugged, a sheepish grin on his face.

"It's true, and I won't deny it. Paris said if I gave *Emma* a chance, I'd find something to enjoy. She wasn't wrong," Dax said. "Austen's sharp wit and keen insights into human quirks grabbed me. The way she builds her characters, real and flawed, makes them relatable. And the banter between Emma and Mr. Knightley? Sharp as a knife and twice as cutting. I actually laughed out loud. Plus, her take on the upper-class, all that nonsense about status and match-making—it's brilliant. Never thought I'd say this about a romance novel, but *Emma* has substance, and I can appreciate that." Dax's gaze met mine, and he winked.

The sun climbed higher in the sky, its rays beating down on us like an overzealous spotlight. This day would be seared into my memory forever, and it wasn't just the fact that we were discussing 18th-century literature within our own little Austenian world.

Hours later, Carmen, Rachel, Samuel, and Aunt Margo got to their feet. Dax and I lingered on the blanket, while the others gathered their things and said goodbye. Once they had left, I leaned back on my hands and stretched out my legs.

"I can't believe you pulled all this together." Dax pointed at the empty plastic dishes and paper lanterns swaying overhead in the trees.

Shrugging, I was pleased he appreciated the details. "I wanted to give you the full immersive experience. Though I'll admit, it was as much for me as it was for you and the book club."

"Well, then consider me immersed."

We lapsed into a comfortable silence. I glanced at his profile, admiring the play of light and shadow across his handsome features.

"What?" Dax asked, catching my stare.

"Oh, just thinking about the book club and how much fun today was."

He picked at a blade of grass. "At first I was skeptical about this whole romance novel thing, but you were right... there's a lot more to the storylines than I realized."

His stare held mine and butterflies erupted in my belly. Before I could think better of it, I reached out and placed my hand over his where it rested on the blanket. Dax turned his palm upward to link his fingers through mine.

"How about a little test on those romance tropes we discussed? For instance, what did you make of the 'misunderstanding that could've been solved with a single conversation' trope in *Emma*?"

"Ah, the classic trap of romance," Dax said. "It's the backbone of suspense in love stories, right? Keeps you hooked, waiting to see how it all gets sorted out." Dax shifted closer, his gaze dropping to my lips. "However, some misunderstandings are better resolved...not with words, but with actions." He untangled our fingers and scooted closer until he was right beside me.

"*Oh?* Really?" A goofy, stupid grin lifted my lips. "For instance?"

Dax closed the distance between us, and his lips met mine in a gentle kiss, then passion flared, and the kiss deepened, sending a rush of heat through me. The softness of his mouth against mine, the firm grip of his hand holding my waist, all thoughts dissolved except the sensation of being wholly, completely kissed.

I melted into his embrace, inhaling the intoxicating

scent of his masculine cologne. His fingers gripped my hip tighter, and I tangled my hands in his wavy hair, pulling him closer. The world around us vanished until there was nothing but this perfect moment, this incredible connection, and the all-consuming need to lose myself entirely in his touch, his taste, his arms.

As the kissing intensified, so did a nagging voice within me—a reminder that kisses often led to heartbreak. A lump formed in my throat, thick and unyielding. I quickly pulled back, my breathing shallow like a struggle against an invisible chokehold.

Dax frowned. "Did I overstep? Because if I—"

"No, no, it's not you. It's just..." I hesitated and my mouth dried. "After what happened before, I'm scared of getting hurt again. I don't know if I'm ready to take that risk, even though I'm attracted to you and I love spending time with you." I took a deep breath, trying to steady my voice. "I really value our friendship, and I couldn't handle losing you. You're like the peanut butter to my jelly, the Darcy to my Elizabeth, the...well, you get the idea."

He shifted to face me fully. "I understand. Trust me, I do. But can't we give it a chance? See where this goes?" His voice was low, gruff.

Within me, a maelstrom of emotions threatened to spill over and I tugged at my sash. "What if we're just setting ourselves up for disappointment? What if we're like two mismatched socks, never meant to be?"

Dax wore a half-smile. "I know you've been burned in the past, and I could kill those guys for hurting you—but that's *not* me. And I want more, more than just friendship. I said I'd give you time to think and I have. Now I need to know if this is happening...because, Paris Novak, I'm crazy about you."

His confession hung in the air, an enticing promise of something deeper, something real. Could I take that leap of trust? Risk my heart on the chance that Dax might not hurt me?

I searched his face, desperately seeking any hint of deception, any reason to doubt him. There was none. Only a raw, honest vulnerability that caused my breath to hitch in my throat.

A part of me soared at the thought of an *us*, yet fear lingered. The back of my throat burned with unshed tears, bitter and acrid, making it difficult to swallow. Gambling our friendship for a relationship that might end badly—it was like playing Russian roulette with my heart.

"I'm so sorry, Dax, but I only want to be friends. I can't risk our friendship on a *maybe*." My voice wavered, betraying the conflict twisting and turning within me.

Dax's hands clenched at his sides. "I think you're lying to yourself."

"What?"

"Paris..." Dax's voice softened, but the intensity in his stare held steady. "I've read more romance this past month than in my entire life. Not just because it's your favorite genre, but because I wanted to understand what makes you tick. To make you happy. And yeah, our day-to-day couldn't be more different, but..." He trailed off and got to his feet. "Look, I'm not asking for forever here. Just a shot. But if that's too much to gamble, then I'll back off."

Them my thoughts flashed through every romance trope, trying to find our fit. Were we friends-to-lovers or opposites attract? Or two characters destined to remain on separate pages? I groaned. Did it matter? Yes, yes it did. I would forever be the cautious, overthinking bookshop owner tethered firmly to the ground.

"I appreciate you reading those books, for trying, but I need time. It's not a *no*, just a...not right now."

"You're scared," Dax said, his voice strained. "Scared of what this could be, of how it might change things. Paris, I'll never hurt you."

I stood up, smoothing down my dress. "It's not that simple."

"I haven't been able to get you out of my head. Your passion for books, the way your face lights up when you talk about your favorites, the scent of your peach shampoo that lingers whenever you're near. I find myself constantly wanting to talk to you, to be around you." Dax stepped closer. "You're the only person I can't wait to talk to every day. I see you, Paris. The real *you*. And when it comes to something I really want, something I believe in, well, I'm not afraid to lay it all on the line."

My heart stuttered. This was the moment in every romance novel where the heroine either ran into the hero's arms or ran away. I wasn't sure which path to choose.

"What if we're just setting ourselves up for heartbreak?" I whispered.

Dax's hand cupped my cheek. "And what if this is the start of something amazing?"

I jerked back. "I told you, I'm not sure I'm ready. That this is a good idea. Why can't things just stay the way they are?"

Dax threw his hands up. "I'm not going to stand here and argue with you—convince you to be with me. Maybe William was right. Maybe this"—he gestured between us—"is just a pipe dream. And if that's how you feel, then perhaps it's best that we end this before it even begins."

Staring at him, a prickling sensation burned my eyes. "I think you're right."

His shoulders slumped, the fight draining out of him. "Yeah, maybe I am."

He turned on his heel and walked away.

It felt like my heart had been ripped from my chest, leaving a gaping, raw wound in its place. Every breath I took was painful, as if the jagged edges of the hole were scraping against my lungs.

That naive, eternally optimistic side of me wanted to believe love could conquer all, just like in the pages of my favorite romance novels. The wiser part of me, the part that had been bruised by past heartbreaks, knew better. In the end, no matter how much we cared for each other, our paths were destined to diverge. Letting him go now would spare me greater pain down the road. Better to end things before we became too deeply entangled. Before I lost myself completely.

But why did I want to chase after him? Why was every step he took away from me like a dagger twisting in my chest? Why did it feel like I was willfully ripping out the pages of my own love story?

My throat constricted. What would Emma do?

Probably not stand here feeling sorry for herself, that's for sure. With a sigh, I gathered the blankets and leftovers, then shuffled home to drown my sorrows in chocolate crois-sants and cat cuddles.

# Chapter Sixteen

THE SUNDAY AFTERNOON SUN BEAMED THROUGH the windows of Prose & Positivity onto the worn wooden floors. The aroma of pastries and fresh coffee wafted in the air.

Sitting on a chair in the reading nook, I was ready for the Literary Persuasion Society book club. Earlier today I had texted the group chat, needing the comfort of my bookshop for this get-together.

Carmen was the first to breeze inside. "*Querida*, what's the urgency?" She eased into an armchair, a batik blouse and paint-splattered pants draping her figure.

Samuel followed with a to-go cup of coffee in his hand. "Hope I haven't missed any scandalous confessions." He lowered himself into a seat.

"Not yet," I said. "I wanna wait until everyone is here."

Rachel entered next, in a purple button-up sweater and skirt ensemble, and plopped on a chair. "Spill the tea, Paris. I had to cancel my crochet club's competitive yarn-off to rush over here."

Aunt Margo strutted through the door, trailing scarves

and bangles. She sat next to me, her paisley skirt flaring out. "My star charts revealed big news today."

"All right, everyone, gather round. Emergency meeting at Prose & Positivity!"

While my friends settled into their usual spots, I was hit by a sudden fluster of nerves. This was a big moment for me, a revelation that went against everything I thought I understood about myself as a reader.

I took a deep breath, steeling myself for the reactions that were sure to come. "I have a confession to make...I think I might like reading horror."

The room erupted in a chorus of gasps and exclamations. Rachel froze with a hand covering her mouth. Samuel nearly choked on his coffee, coughing and sputtering. Carmen's eyebrows shot up, disappearing beneath her wispy bangs.

Aunt Margo laughed. "Honey, have you been abducted by aliens and reprogrammed?"

I got it. It was surprising. Me, the queen of happily-ever-afters and swoony romances enjoying horror, of all things. It was like discovering I liked sardines on pizza or I could rock a neon green fanny pack. Unthinkable, and yet...

"Ha-ha," I said. "No alien abductions. I've been reading the books Dax recommended."

Samuel cleared his throat, having recovered from his near-death experience with the coffee. "I must say, Paris, I'm impressed. So you really liked reading the horror genre?"

"Both of the books that Dax assigned me to read had a romance, and honestly, I enjoyed them. Turns out there's more to horror than gratuitous violence and jump scares."

Carmen picked a speck of paint off her arm. "Ah, the influence of a certain horror-loving hunk. I bet Dax is thrilled to have a new convert to his literary tastes."

"What's your favorite so far?" Rachel asked, leaning forward in her seat.

"Probably *It's Alive!*. It was so much more than just a monster story. It had these layers of existential dread and complex character development that I never expected."

Samuel stroked his chin. "I've heard good things about that one. Might have to add it to my reading list."

Carmen pursed her lips. "Paris Novak recommending horror novels. And will you be hosting a Halloween party at the bookshop this year?"

Shrugging, I smirked. "Could be. I'm still new to this whole horror thing."

Aunt Margo grinned wickedly. "I'm suddenly reminded of when Paris was a little girl."

I groaned inwardly, bracing myself for whatever embarrassing childhood anecdote she was about to unleash.

"Paris was six-years-old, curled up on the couch with her favorite stuffed bunny. We were watching TV together, waiting for a Disney movie to start."

My cheeks heated up, knowing exactly where this story was headed.

"A trailer for this new horror movie comes on. I think it was called *The Attack of the Garden Gnomes* or something like that. And Paris took one look at the screen and let out a blood-curdling scream."

The room erupted in laughter, and I buried my face in my hands.

"Paris was so scared, she ran out of the room and hid under her bed. I had to coax her out with promises of extra dessert and a new book," Aunt Margo said.

My hands lifted in surrender. "Okay, okay. In my defense, those garden gnomes were terrifying. And I was six!"

Rachel giggled. "Aww, little Paris, afraid of the big bad elves."

"Gnomes. And hey, I've come a long way since then," I said.

"*Querida*, this reminds me of when I first started exploring watercolors," Carmen said. "I was so skeptical at first, but once I opened my mind to the possibilities, it was like a whole new talent opened up to me." She fixed me with a meaningful look, her voice taking on a more serious tone. "Sometimes, the things we resist the most are the things that have the most to teach us. About the world, and ourselves."

Rachel's expression turned serious. "I think you should share this with Dax."

I blinked. "Share what?"

"The way you've opened your mind to new genres, new ideas. I think Dax would be proud of you," Rachel said.

"You think so?"

It was true, Dax had challenged me to step outside my literary comfort zone. Who would have thought a simple genre swap could lead to a full-blown existential crisis—book style? I was a seasoned romance aficionado, who now read horror, and learning to sleep with the lights on—just in case.

"And look at you now," Rachel said, "boldly going where no book matchmaker has gone before."

Samuel nodded. "And this could be the start of something more between you two kids. Frankly, I'm surprised that boy hasn't asked you to be his girlfriend. Especially the way, he's been mooning over you like a lovesick puppy for months."

Glancing at the motley crew of booklovers, my stomach roiled. This meeting wasn't just about sharing my latest literary epiphany, no, it was about Dax, the cute personal trainer who'd wormed his way into my genre preferences and possibly my heart.

"Um, about that..." I fiddled with a loose thread on my graphic tee, today's slogan: *Books Are My Happy Place.* Taking a deep breath, I said, "Dax did ask if I wanted to take our relationship to the next level, to make things official between us."

My admission hung in the air like a cliffhanger waiting for resolution. The book club members leaned in, all smiles and wide stares.

"And?" Rachel's eyebrows raised so high they nearly disappeared into her hairline. "Don't leave us hanging, Paris! What did you say?"

A knot formed in my stomach. "Um, well, I told him I needed time to think about it. Don't get me wrong, Dax is amazing, but diving into a full-blown relationship is scarier than a Shirley Jackson novel."

Aunt Margo merely smiled as if she had seen this coming all along. "It was written in the stars, honey."

"It was obvious, *querida,* he likes you very much," Carmen said.

Rachel squeezed my hand. "Anyone with eyes can see the chemistry between you and Dax. You're like the perfect opposites attract love story."

My chest tightened suddenly and I couldn't breathe. There were so many reasons why dating Dax was a terrible idea. What if he broke my heart? Or I hurt him?

Thoughts of Julian's deception flooded my mind, reminding me of the pain I'd endured. My skin prickled with a cold sweat, as if my body was trying to purge itself of the toxic memories that clung to every pore. I couldn't bear the thought of experiencing that kind of heartbreak again, of allowing myself to be vulnerable. It might be stupid, but the fear of history repeating itself kept me guarded, hesitant to take a chance on love, even if it meant missing out on something potentially wonderful.

Even as I tried to convince myself this was the right choice, doubt crept in. The thought of a future without Dax stretched before me, bleak and colorless. Despite my best efforts to keep him at arm's length, he'd somehow snuck past my defenses, planting seeds of hope I couldn't seem to uproot. Now I wondered if I was making the biggest mistake of my life, letting my fears and past wounds dictate my future. A future I might have with Dax...

"*Erm*, I, uh, told him that I just wanted to be friends." I fidgeted with the hem of my shirt, avoiding everyone's curious stare. "Because if it doesn't work out, it'll ruin our friendship." I looked at Rachel. "And I know you said that would never happen since we're so close, but I can't know that for sure...and I might've already screwed things up with my indecisiveness. I mean, I like Dax. I'm attracted to him. But what if we're better off as friends? I don't know if I can handle losing him completely if things go south."

I took a shaky breath, my head hurting from all these conflicting thoughts. On one hand, the idea of being with Dax filled me with a dizzy excitement. His smile, his laugh, the way he looked at me like I was the only person in the world...it all made me happy in the best possible way. But on the other hand, the fear of getting hurt again, of opening myself up only to be left broken and betrayed, weighed heavily on my heart.

Yep, I was a hot, indecisive mess.

Aunt Margo placed a hand on my knee. "Honey, you've been hurt in the past and it's okay to be cautious, but this is Dax."

Rachel nodded. "Dax is a good man and he cares about you."

My cat jumped down from a bookshelf and hopped onto my lap. Sighing, I absently stroked Sushi's soft fur. "I...I'm scared."

Samuel cleared his throat, adjusting his glasses. "Paris, I've only ever loved one woman, my late wife. And let me tell you, that kind of love, it's rare. When you find it, you gotta grab onto it and never let go."

"I'm not an expert on love," Aunt Margo said. "But not taking a chance on something real, that's the kinda regret that eats away at you. My fourth husband has his faults—he's a terrible interpretive dancer—and we certainly have our differences, but it wouldn't stop me from marrying him all over again."

Aunt Margo had a point. Maybe I was overthinking everything, as usual.

Sushi meowed as if agreeing with my aunt and sprang off my lap.

Carmen smiled softly. "And I think Dax is a good match for you. Don't let fear hold you back."

I took a deep, shaky breath. "I hear you all. I do, but...but what if I'm just not cut out for this? What if I'm meant to be alone with my books and cat?"

In response, my fluffy white overlord purred, winding herself around my ankles as if to reassure me I'd never be alone, not really.

Samuel cleared his throat. "Well, maybe you should write your own story. Plus, who says you can't have books, cats, and love?"

I huffed out a breath. "Yeah, but this isn't a novel. In real life, there's no author making sure everything works out with a tidy happy ending."

Rachel gave me a no-nonsense look and said, "Listen up, girl. You and Dax? You complement each other. He pushes you to be bold, to color outside the lines, and to embrace life beyond these four walls. It's like he's the key that's unlocked a whole new side of you, one that's been waiting for a good man to come along and give it a good kick in the pants. So, stop overthinking it."

I groaned as more excuses poured from my mouth. "What if our differences are too big to overcome? Look at our reading preferences. He loves horror, I love romance. He eats healthy and I live on donuts. We're like oil and water."

"That's just it," Aunt Margo said, her tone gentle but firm. "Being diverse is okay. What one person enjoys, another may not. Just because you appreciate different genres, and foods, and have wildly contrasting opinions on the proper way to hang toilet paper rolls, doesn't mean you can't find common ground."

My throat tightened with emotion. As much as I hated to admit it, they had a reasonable argument. Dax wasn't just some random guy trying to sweep me off my feet with empty promises and grand gestures. He was becoming my best friend, my sounding board, my...well, my *everything*.

My heart pinched in an already sore place. I had already fallen for a guy who I thought was the one, and it turned out he was engaged to someone else the whole time. It had shattered me, and I'd been too scared to trust my heart since then. Now I was letting fear keep me from a relationship. It was like I was the protagonist in one of those frustrating romance novels, where you just want to shake some sense into the heroine and tell her to go for it already.

Carmen leaned in, her voice gentle. "You've got a heart

big enough to love deeply. Don't let the past keep you from experiencing that."

Sushi meowed and sprang onto the counter, her tail swishing.

My heart constricted, and their heartfelt advice started chipping away at all of my doubts and fears. They were right. Dax liked me for who I was, always cheering me on, and supporting my dreams. He understood me in a way no one else ever had.

The truth was, I'd been running from love for so long, I'd forgotten what it felt like to be truly seen, to be understood on a soul-deep level.

The awareness of my own stubborn foolishness came crashing down on me, like a hardback. Dax and I might be different in so many ways, but that didn't have to be a bad thing. In fact, it could be the very thing that made us stronger.

I wrung my hands. "I don't know what to do now. What if I've ruined everything by keeping him in the friend zone? What if Dax doesn't want to give me another chance?"

"You won't know unless you try. Trust your heart," Rachel said.

A watery smile lifted my mouth. "I've been a fool, haven't I? Pushing away the one person who truly gets me, who sees past my neuroses and still wants to stick around, who makes me giggle until I snort-laugh and doesn't even judge me for it."

Aunt Margo clapped her hands together. "Yes, honey! I told you, the stars are aligned in your favor."

Okay, so it was time to stop overthinking and start living. I'd been so wrapped up in my own insecurities that I'd lost sight of what really mattered—the chance to build something amazing with Dax. Clearly, there were no guarantees in life, but wasn't that what made it so interesting?

I sat up straighter. "I'm going to talk to Dax. Tell him how I feel, how much he means to me. And if he's willing to give me another chance, I'll even read all of his favorite horror novels, as long as he agrees to discuss them over raspberry tarts."

Rachel punched a fist into the air. "Go get your man, girl. And don't forget to come back and tell us all the juicy details!"

I faced the book club members, my found family. A swell of affection and belonging struck me. These were my people, my tribe. They might be an opinionated bunch, but also, the most loyal, loving friends a girl could ask for.

"Thank you, all of you. For believing in me, even when I didn't believe in myself."

Samuel grinned, his eyes crinkling behind his glasses. "That's what we're here for, Paris. Now, go get your happily ever after."

I didn't know what Dax would do or say when I talked to him, but I knew I was done running from love.

# Chapter Seventeen

*Dax*

THE GYM WAS FILLED WITH PEOPLE WHOSE LIVES I'd helped change and I was ready to do even more now that I owned the gym. I grinned, leaning against the freshly polished counter.

My thoughts shifted from workouts to genre debates to that cute bookshop owner. At first, swapping out hard-boiled thrillers and horror for sappy love stories with Paris had felt like nails on a chalkboard. With each book, those stories started chipping away at the calloused exterior I'd been hiding behind for years. I was done playing games and finally ready to go all-in—to take charge of my life.

I hadn't gotten the girl, but at least I had accomplished my dream.

"Daxton, if you spend any more time daydreaming out that window, I'll charge you rent for the view." Tom Granger, my father, who wore a white button-up shirt untucked over slacks, walked behind the counter.

"Trust me, Dad, the only thing I'm focused on right

now is this place." I gestured to the expanse of workout machines and free weights.

This gym was more than a business transaction, it was a dream molded from sweat and ambition, now tangible in every dumbbell and treadmill.

His smile widened. "Good." He clasped my shoulder with a firm hand. "I'm happy to help, Daxton, and not just because I'm charging you interest on this loan."

Rolling my eyes, I glanced at the signed paperwork spread before us. "I can't thank you enough, Dad. I have big plans for improvements and offering workout therapy classes next month."

"I think you'll do well." Dad raised an eyebrow. "Ah, may I ask about the girl you've been spending so much time with? What was her name, Paris?—the one who owns the bookshop. Your mother wants to meet her."

My face heated up despite the cool air of the gym. "Yeah, we still hang out. But she made it clear we're only friends. It's all good though—I'm glad to have her in my life, even if it's not the way that I had hoped."

"That's a mature way to look at it, son. Whatever happens, you've got my full support. I'm proud of how you're handling things, in business and in your personal life."

My father's belief in me only anchored my resolve. With his backing, both financial and paternal, the path forward seemed a little less daunting now that I owned The Muscle Hut.

Dad clasped my hand in a solid shake, the deal sealed, the future bright. "Now, go make the most of it, Daxton."

With a final nod, he strode out of the gym, leaving me to relish in the glow of ambitions becoming reality. And somewhere between the clinking of weights and the steady tempo of treadmills, a flow of pride straightened my posture. I had fulfilled my goal of becoming a businessowner. It was a risk, but standing here felt like it was exactly where I was meant to be.

The door swung open, and William entered, his gym bag slung over one shoulder. The guy was built like a tank, and his closely cropped hair was reminiscent of a soldier fresh out of boot camp.

"Morning, Dax," he greeted me.

"Hey, Will."

"You're here earlier than usual. What's the matter? Hanging out at Paris's bookstore not cutting it anymore?" He glanced at the paperwork and the deed to the gym still on the counter. "What's this?"

I leaned over the front desk. "I purchased the gym today. You work for me now."

"Damn, buddy. Good for you." He switched the gym bag to the other shoulder. "Does that mean I get a raise?"

I chuckled. "No. But you can take on a few of my clients to help ease the load."

"You still seeing Paris?" He said it as if it left a bad taste in his mouth.

My hands clenched at my sides. "I don't get you. Paris is best friends with your wife. Explain why you don't like her because your answer is going to decide whether we stay friends."

William heaved a sigh. "Lately, Rachel's all wrapped up in her books and that book club, and she barely notices me. And now you're always with Paris. Look, I'm not trying to be a jerk. I want you to be happy, to find someone great...I just worry you're gonna cut me out of your life, that's all."

I grunted. "Wow. To think the mighty William is afraid of a little competition."

"Shut up," he grumbled, but there was a hint of sheepishness in his voice.

Slapping a hand on his shoulder with a firm grip, I said, "Listen up, Will. Paris isn't gonna take anyone's place. She's just...she opened my eyes to things I never gave a chance to before and I enjoy her company." I frowned at him. "And free advice? If you want to rekindle your relationship with your wife, why not join the book club? I'm sure Rachel would love that."

"Yeah, yeah." William gripped a dumbbell. "All right then, Romeo. Let's see if this newfound perspective has improved your deadlift."

We worked out together in comfortable silence, our earlier conflict dissolving with each lift and press. Pushing through the sets, I let my mind wander to Paris—the catalyst for all this change—and how the courage gleaned from fictional happy endings might help me find one of my own.

After finishing our session with record weights and high fives that were only slightly ironic, we ambled toward the locker room.

Sitting on the bench, I sighed. "Purchasing this gym...it was actually Paris who inspired me to finally do it."

William, still catching his breath, gave me a quizzical look. "How'd she get you to do that?"

"One night while we were hanging out, she shared how she'd always dreamt of making her bookshop a landmark in Bluebell Bend, and how she wanted to be a book influencer. It made me think about my own dreams and how I'd been sitting on this gym idea for too long."

William took a sip from his water bottle. "Well, I'm glad some good came out of this genre-swapping nonsense. I suppose she's been a good influence on you and I misjudged her."

"Ya think?" I grunted, shaking my head. "Being around Paris, seeing how she doesn't cave to expectations but thrives on being herself is inspiring. She also got me into genres I never considered before—like romance."

"Keep your voice down." William cracked a smile. "Just don't tell me you want to start double-dating at poetry slams on Thursday nights."

Laughing, I dropped my hand from his shoulder. "Could be, buddy. But Paris and I are just friends, no dating."

William set his bottle down. "Ah, I'm sorry, dude. I know you really like her."

I shrugged. "It's all good." Not really. I was crushed and hurt and still grieving, but putting on a brave face.

"Maybe I should give one of those romance novels a try."

Now it was my turn to be surprised. "You serious?"

He scratched his head. "Why not? It's all my wife reads, so yeah."

I chuckled and promised to lend him one from my own collection at home—a gesture of brotherhood forged in sweat and literary confessions.

William nodded slowly. "Seems Paris has had quite the effect on you."

Paris had bulldozed through my life like a wrecking ball, leaving me exposed but somehow stronger. She'd challenged me to flex muscles I didn't even know I had—not the physical kind, but the ones that make you stand tall in your own skin. It was like spotting for someone at the gym and realizing you're the one getting stronger. Weird how a bookworm could teach a gym rat new tricks about personal growth.

I nodded. "She has, more than I ever expected. It's

about owning who you are, and embracing what makes you different. She helped me see that being myself, a gym-loving book nerd, and horror fan, isn't just okay—it's something to celebrate. I owe her a lot." I stood up. "For now, I'll start by making this gym a standout place, I've got a lot of big ideas for improvements."

"I wish you every success, buddy. Not that you're gonna need it."

After giving William a manly half-hug and agreeing to meet up for some brews later in the week, a realization hit me like a ton of barbells.

This whole reading challenge thing had been my brain-child—a way to get to know a pretty girl that kicked off months ago. Somewhere along the way, it had morphed into a wild ride of self-discovery, and now, I hardly recognized the man staring back at me in the mirror. I was a businessowner now, running my own show and calling the shots. I'd leveled up in a big way, but a nagging feeling crept in. The sense that something was missing, like I needed someone by my side to truly appreciate how far I'd come. Someone like Paris...

As I stuffed my gear into my gym bag and yanked the zipper closed, I couldn't ignore the cold, hard truth—Paris had laid her cards on the table, and I had to respect that.

With a resolute nod, I squared my shoulders and headed out, knowing deep down that whatever the future held for us, our friendship was too damn valuable to let slip away.

# Chapter Eighteen

While I stood behind the front counter, halfheartedly sorting through a stack of newly arrived books, I cringed at the hot mess I'd created. Trust me to have a rom-com worthy epiphany that I was head over heels, crazy in love with Dax Granger...right after I'd friend-zoned him.

Talk about impeccable timing!

I'd spent so long convincing myself that Dax and I were just friends, two polar opposites—me with my dog-eared paperbacks and him with his fancy eReader—I never noticed how well we clicked despite our differences. How I had put up high walls to keep myself save, guarded. That my fear of being hurt again had closed me off to letting go and moving on. Now looking back, I must have been falling in love with him all along. I was just too stubborn to see it until now.

Dax had become my best friend and favorite person. He made me laugh like no one else could and accepted my quirks. Even when we disagreed, he always listened and respected my opinions.

Through our endless conversations about books, life, and everything in between, Dax had shown me the strength and value of opening up and letting someone in. We shared a bond that went beyond just two people who loved to read.

I paced back and forth. "How could I have messed this up so badly? How could I have been so blind? Too hard-headed to see what was right in front of me?"

Sushi lounged on a stack of hardcovers. "Meow," she said as if to remind me that she'd known all along that I was too pragmatic.

I sighed, blowing out a breath. "I know, I know. I'm an idiot."

And I had given him more mixed signals than a broken traffic light. So, if he only wanted to stay friends after all the confusion I caused, I wouldn't blame him.

Sushi tilted her head, her green eyes narrowing.

Scooping her up, I nuzzled her soft fur. "I may be a hopeless romantic on paper, but apparently I'm clueless in real life." Setting Sushi down, tears lined my eyes. "I owe Dax an apology for being so oblivious. And a thank you for being so patient with me while I figured it out...I have to tell Dax how I feel before it's too late."

Lost in thought, I barely noticed when the bookshop door swung open. Dax strode inside with an adorably nervous smile on his face. My pulse kicked into overdrive.

"Hi, um, how are you?"

He took a step forward. "I'm good. Really good."

"It's nice to see you, but I thought after our fight..."

"That I didn't want to be friends anymore?" He smiled. "How can I end a friendship where we complete each other's sentences? Now that's rare."

My heart did a little happy dance like it had just won

the lottery and was now off to buy a lifetime supply of chocolate and books.

"So, you're really not mad at me?"

"Of course not, bookworm. And I come bearing news." He puffed out his chest. "I bought The Muscle Hut. You're looking at the proud owner of a gym. Now I'm more than just a pretty face, I'm a businessowner."

"Congratulations! I always knew you had it in you." I moved around the counter and gave him a quick hug. And damn he smelled good.

Dax grinned. "I couldn't have done it without your support and encouragement. You believed in me even when I doubted myself."

"So, does this mean you'll be too busy pumping iron and looking over accounting spreadsheets to hang out with little ole me?"

He moved a little closer. "I'll always make time for you. Besides, I need someone to keep me humble amidst all the muscle worship."

"Oh, I think I can manage that." I gave his upper-arm a gentle squeeze. "Wouldn't want your head getting bigger than your biceps, now would we?"

Dax laughed. I loved the way his face lit up when he smiled. It was a sight I could never tire of.

"Just promise me one thing," I said. "Don't go replacing me with some fitness influencer now that you're a bigshot gym owner."

"*Never.* You'll always be the bookmark to my book, Paris."

My heart started missing some beats and doubling others, unable to find a regular rhythm. "*Aww,* you really know how to charm a girl with bookish metaphors. Keep that up, and I might just swoon."

"Well, lucky for you, I'm good at catching swooning bookworms."

For a moment, I couldn't breathe, couldn't think of anything except the way Dax was looking at me as if I were the answer to a question he'd been asking his entire life.

He cleared his throat. "Look, I know you just want to be friends and I'm okay with it. And I know we come from different worlds, different tastes in books and all that. But the more time I spend with you, the more I realize that none of that matters. What matters is how I feel when I'm with you...as your friend. So, yeah, I'd like to keep being a part of your life, in whatever way you're comfortable with."

I gazed up at him, his hazel eyes glittering with flecks of gold in the light of the bookshop. "There's something I need you to know...something I should've told you sooner. Before I met you, I was content living vicariously through characters in books, but you've shown me there's more to life than hiding behind a stack of Austen novels."

A slow, crooked smile spread across Dax's face. "Is that so?" he murmured, his voice deep and husky.

Biting my lip, I tried to gather my thoughts. Being this close to him made my brain go fuzzy. "You've dared me to step outside my comfort zone, to take chances, and to take a risk on..." I trailed off, my cheeks heating under his intense gaze.

He stepped closer, looking down at me. "What, Paris?"

"Love," I whispered. "I've been a fool, Dax. I've been so focused on our differences and my own insecurities that I didn't see how perfectly we complement each other, and how much you mean to me.."

He gazed deeply into my eyes. "Are you saying...are you sure, bookworm?"

"I was too scared to take a chance before," I said, my

voice hoarse with emotion. "I know I can be a stubborn pain in the butt sometimes, but I can't imagine my life without you. I'm sorry it took me so long to realize it, but I'm crazy in love with you. So, yes, I'm sure. I'm sure about us, if you'll still have me."

"Damn, it's good to hear you say that." Dax pulled me flush against his muscular chest. The heat of his body seeped through his clothes, and my skin tingled. "I've been falling for you since the moment we met, even when we were bickering about books," he murmured, his expression warm with affection. "You're the most passionate, intelligent, and beautiful woman I've ever known. I want to be by your side, to support you, and to make you laugh, if you feel the same."

"Dax, I do feel the same way. That's what I've been trying to say!" Tears blurred my eyes, and I blinked them away, not wanting to miss a moment of this. "You've shown me what it means to truly connect with someone, to share hopes, dreams, and to trust again. I never thought I could feel this way about anyone, but with you, it's like...it's like I'm finally home."

He drew me closer, his forehead resting against mine, his breath warm on my skin. "You've taught me there's strength in vulnerability and love is about opening your heart and letting someone see all of you, even the messy, imperfect parts. And I..." He swallowed hard, his voice dropping to a whisper. "I love every part of you, Paris. Every eccentric, wonderful, maddening inch."

"I love you too, Dax." I wrapped my arms around him, gazing up into his face.

Dax's lips curved into a tender smile, and he leaned down, his forehead resting against mine. My heart swelled with a love so fierce, it stole my breath. My arms slid around his neck, pulling him down into a mind-blowing kiss. His hands slipped down my back to pull me impossibly closer as I leaned into his embrace. The kiss became more passionate and intense. My skin felt hypersensitive, every graze of his mouth and caress of his hands amplified my love for him.

As we lost ourselves in each other, surrounded by the aroma of books and coffee, my heart got all giddy. This moment, this feeling...it was better than anything I could have ever read in a novel. Because it was real, and it was ours.

When we finally parted, breathless and flushed, a smile lifted my kiss-swollen lips.

He kissed my forehead. "Is this what Emma would do?"

"I think she would approve. After all, even the most unlikely matches can lead to the most epic love stories."

Dax lowered his head and I closed my eyes, loving the sensation of being held by him. Our lips met in another kiss and it was like we were discovering each other on the deepest, most intimate level. His arms, strong and firm, pulled me tight against his chest. I tangled my fingers in his thick hair, and deepened the kiss. His hands roamed my back, and I lost myself in the emotion and sensation, ready to surrender completely to the love and longing that had lain dormant within me for so long.

At that moment, nothing else mattered—not the bookshop, not the world outside, not even the purring cat watching us from the bookshelf.

When we came up for air, I glimpsed a future stretching out before us where our differences were not obstacles but opportunities, where the power of opposites attracting led to the magic that happens when two unlikely souls find each other within a judgy small town.

Dax grinned. "You know, bookworm, I'm starting to

think that romance novels have gotten it right all along. Because with you, I feel like I'm living in one of those stories you love so much."

I laughed, playfully swatting his chest. "Just wait until we have to deal with the dramatic misunderstandings and cliffhanger endings," I teased.

He pulled me closer, his voice low and filled with promise. "I wouldn't have it any other way. You and me, we're in this for the long haul. No matter what plot twists life throws our way. Because that's what real love is all about."

I smiled, my heart overflowing with love and happiness. In my little bookshop, surrounded by the very walls that had brought two friends together, I'd found my happily ever after.

If you want to be notified when Sherry Sinclair's next novel is released or whenever she's offering free reads, please sign up for her newsletter to be notified of new releases, giveaways, and free reads by clicking: https://dashboard.mailerlite.com/forms/748734/109192166606112621/share (*Your email will never be shared, and you can unsubscribe at any time.*)

# Pride & Property

**THE PERSON, BE IT GENTLEMAN OR LADY, WHO has not pleasure in a good novel and a quiet writing spot, must be intolerably noisy...**

In the height of summer in the small town of Honeysuckle Hollow, Briar Quinn—author and Austen aficionado—plans to pen her next literary masterpiece in serene solitude. But when the incessant noise from a nearby construction site shatters her concentration, she's determined to halt the disruptive development. To her shock, the man behind the chaos is none other than her high school sweetheart—the one who broke her heart and stole her English notes.

Drake Winslow, a charming yet brazen real estate developer and modern-day Wentworth (if he bulldozed historic homes), is eager to replace the town's old Victorians with sleek, modern homes. Armed with a seemingly inexhaustible supply of gourmet coffee bribes for the town council, he's not about to let a bookish ex-girlfriend stand in his way.

When Drake's grand plans for a neighborhood makeover collide with Briar's desperate need for peace and quiet, they find themselves entangled in a battle of wits, wills, and scorching chemistry. From their first calamitous encounter involving a raccoon to the fate of the neighborhood, Briar and Drake discover that the heart's blueprint doesn't always follow plan.

*Is it possible for a bulldozer and a wordsmith to learn that the best second chances are the ones you never see coming?*

# The Sweetest Ingredient

**IT IS A TRUTH UNIVERSALLY ACKNOWLEDGED
that a baker in possession of a good fortune must be in
want of a sassy flirt...**

When Kenzi Middleton, an out-of-work graphic
designer and Jane Austen fangirl, steps into Doughy

Desires, she expects an awkward blind date, not a job interview. Talk about mixed signals! With financial pressures mounting, Kenzi sees this twist of fate as a much-needed lifeline.

Which is why Kenzi lies through her teeth to the broodingly gorgeous bakery owner, Mr. Darcy, erm—Bishop Caine about her baking experience. Or lack thereof. And Kenzi knows she should absolutely not be crushing on her new boss, she has enough trouble discerning sugar from salt.

Yet despite Bishop's gruff demeanor and the pressure of false pretenses, they ignite a passion hotter than any oven. But just as Kenzi starts to weaken his stern exterior, family drama, spiteful rumors, and a cutthroat bake-off threaten their budding romance.

If only Kenzi can get around the deceit of her baking bluff, then she just might have a chance at happiness...

*Will mixing flour and feelings lead to a recipe for disaster, or can love prove the sweetest ingredient of all?*

# Romance, Lies, & Sorority Ties

**REESE HARRINGTON IS A COMPULSIVE LIAR,
*who just wants to escape her shameful past...***

Transferring to a new university her sophomore year, Reese is ready to put the painful past behind her, pledge a sorority, and never date again.

But after befriending Cole Prescott—an annoyingly,

gorgeous complication—her newfound resolve crumbles. Keeping him in the "friend zone" isn't easy, especially when the sizzling chemistry between them is so damn combustible. Except that's not Reese's biggest problem.

While pledging Zeta Beta, her life becomes a nightmare of hazing rituals, nasty rumors, and vicious blackmail. The only place she finds comfort is in the arms of the off-limits frat boy she should be avoiding.

When her darkest secret comes out, can Reese stop lying and finally own the truth?

READ IF YOU LIKE STANDALONE NOVELS WITH high drama, outrageous lies, steamy scenes, and light swears.

# Review Request

more stories filled with love, laughter, and that special spark with you.

Until our next heartfelt encounter,

*~Sherry* (Your ever-grateful author and hopeless romantic)

# About the Author

Sherry Sinclair is the bestselling author of character-driven rom-coms, romantic dramas, and sweet romances, bringing readers the ideal blend of heart, humor, and HEA in every novel. Her books have been called, "bad day cures."

When not crafting happily-ever-afters, Sherry takes on the role of chief can opener and ear scratcher for her cats, who only give her manuscripts approval after plenty of cuddles and treats.

A connoisseur of positivity, she's allergic to gloom and an expert at dodging drama—unless, of course, it's on the page. You might spot Sherry at the gym trying not to trip on the treadmill while plotting her next romantic tale, or lost behind a mountain of books in her to-be-read pile that rivals the local library's stock.

Dear reader, please join Sherry's Facebook group to discuss the romance genre, life, and swap book recommendations: https://www.facebook.com/groups/authorsherrysinclair

Please sign up for my newsletter to be notified of new releases, giveaways, and free reads by clicking: Sherry Sinclair VIP Member (*Your email will never be shared, and you can unsubscribe at any time.*)

Follow Sherry Sinclair on Facebook - Twitter – TikTok – Instagram